PAGOO

BY
HOLLING CLANCY HOLLING

ILLUSTRATED BY THE AUTHOR AND
LUCILLE WEBSTER HOLLING

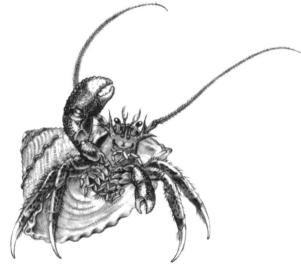

HOUGHTON MIFFLIN COMPANY BOSTON

This book is dedicated to two of the author's smaller-sized cousins,

STEPHEN FREDERICK
and DAVID ADDISON JONES

Stephen sailed in from nowhere to Pasadena, California, dropping anchor within sight of Pagoo's very own ocean. David's craft came to port some three years later at Grinnell, Iowa — where the roll and crash of the sea is apt to be only traffic. This book is really a family affair, because Stephen and David's Grandmother Gertrude is Holling's *first* cousin. Not only that, Grandma Gertrude played, as a girl, with the Lucille of this book, before Lucille knew Holling.

Then Grandma Gertrude grew up, and Marion was her daughter, and Marion grew up in Chicago, by mighty Lake Michigan water. And she married an Addison Jones, and *he* knows about water too, and even how a boat stays on top of it. So Marion and Add are Mother and Dad of Stephen and David who one day may read this *Pagoo* book together.

Printed in the United States of America
RNF ISBN 0-395-06826-6
PAP ISBN 0-395-53964-1

LBM 20 19 18 17 16 15

ACKNOWLEDGMENT

This book provides only a peek into tide-pool life. If it awakens some young reader to further interest in the world under water, Pagoo will have done his bit. We chose this small Hermit Crab as our main character because these clownish creatures are found along the beaches of many seas. We have tried to tell Pagoo's story against a factual background.

The story first was written after studying piecemeal material from a few available publications. Yet these books and pictures failed to answer all questions, so we began collecting specimens, and consulting experts on this coast. Our book being finished, we are indebted to several scientists and other helpful people. Thus, for everything from specimens to sage advice, we wish to thank:

Mr. Sam D. Hinton (artist, writer, noted ballad singer), the Senior Museum Zoologist of the Scripps Institution of Oceanography, at La Jolla, California. He always found the answers, plus material. And an afternoon's collecting jaunt may have been routine for Sam, but his running comments proved invaluable.

Dr. Joel W. Hedgpeth (also at Scripps) had revised a reference work much used by us, *Between Pacific Tides* (Edward F. Ricketts and Jack Calvin). He gave us his compilation *A Preliminary Bibliography of Books on the Seashore, Oceanography and Related Subjects*. It lists hundreds of titles for juvenile and adult.

Dr. John Garth and the Allan Hancock Foundation at the University of Southern California. One of Dr. Garth's graduate students was completing his doctor's thesis on Hermit Crabs, and invited us to watch an immature Pagurus under his microscope. Dr. Garth obtained special permission for our use of the then unpublished thesis data. Thus we rechecked measurements and processes, and the technical diagrams became references for illustrations of Pagoo's early growth. Dr. Garth also found additional material to aid our research. And finally we can thank the writer of the above definitive thesis for his generous assistance, now *Dr. Harold G. Coffin*.

Another of our most important source books is *Natural History of Marine Animals* by George E. and Nettie MacGinitie, of Cal Tech's Kerckhoff Marine Laboratory. For their constructive reading of our story, for their loanings of specimens, for their evenings squandered merely to talk with us—we are most grateful to these friends, the Doctors MacGinitie.

We include a chain-of-connections: Jim Long to Jack Mertz, Announcers, and on to Mr. Ray W. Smith, Vice-President and General Manager of the world's largest Oceanarium at Marineland, California, near San Pedro. This huge modern structure houses giant tanks teeming with salt-water life, including educated porpoises. And, though Marineland's divers, trainers, technicians, scientists, and others may not know it, they have helped this book.

For example, Jake Jacobs had dived as usual to feed fishes on tank bottom, when a nearsighted moray eel mistook his finger for an octopus tentacle, leaving jigsaw lacerations in a spiral. On our first visit we met Jake and Chief Diver Ted Davis as the healing appendage was being dressed. On a later visit to the lab we were still sketching an octopus at closing time when Ted presented us with one freshly defunct, for us to take home; and that octopus ended in this book, pickled in pencil, color, and printer's ink. For octopodal and other courtesies, we thank the entire Oceanarium.

THE AUTHOR AND ILLUSTRATORS

CONTENTS

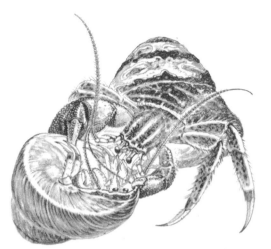

1. PAGOO *MIGHT* BE A HERMIT CRAB

LITTLE Pagurus—"Pagoo" for short—floated at the surface of the sea. Pagurus (Pa-*gu*-rus) would grow into a two-fisted Hermit Crab —if he could make it. Someday he would live near shore, walking on a sea floor of rock and sand. But before he could walk on the sea's bottom he must drift on its top, as helpless as a tiny fleck of foam. Pagoo's chances of growing up were not very good.

Pagoo was quite small, because he had just been hatched from an egg the size of a pencil dot. You could see part way through him— that is, if you first could find his glassy body to slide under a microscope. Whatever he looked like, it certainly was not a two-fisted, happy-go-lucky Hermit Crab, or any other Crab. His large eyes looked like eyes, but the rest of him was all points and joints and fuzzy places. If he had been larger—say, fifty times larger—he might pass as a fancy ornament for a Christmas tree. But he was not up in a tree; he was down in a salty ocean. And Pagoo was too small to add much of a sparkle to the point of a pin.

Pagoo was lucky to be so small, to have a glassy body looking like the water around him, to be almost invisible. In this big ocean, being seen could bring death. Even now, shadows of death swam toward him —gigantic Things almost half an inch long! Behind Pagoo, in front of Pagoo, below, above, on both sides of him the shadowy Things were gliding with mouths wide open. They were swallowing sparkly creatures something like Pagoo, bright flecks in the water which glittered, danced—and then disappeared. Pagoo was only a new-hatched baby, and could not know what was happening. The giant shadows sucked up his shimmering neighbors, somehow passed him by, and little Pagoo was left in the sea with nothing to look at but water.

The water was very nice. In its rocking cradle, Pagoo was content. Though his parents were nowhere near, his "instinct" always would be.

Ancient instinct is a guardian for the very young, who as yet have had no time to learn new things. The young are born with an instinct that tells them what to do, and how to do it. Instinct becomes a trusted pal. So, Pagoo's Old Pal Instinct would pass along the lessons for living, learned by his ancestors long ago in ancient seas. Such advice would come to Pagoo in private Hermit Crab code, but he would understand.

Whole seconds of time passed before Old Pal's message said, "You're *hungry!*" And sure enough, he was. "Try out your mouth parts" set him to moving them. This part went over, that went down —and they all worked. As he pushed his new feathery fronds at the water, Pagoo bumped things like strings of hard-shelled candies. Old Pal Instinct said, "Food," and so Pagoo pushed them into the slot where they should go. Pagoo was eating!

Each diatom (*di*-a-tom) Pagoo ate shimmered with rainbow colors. Though its shell was glassy and brittle, it was a living plant, and Pagoo crunched it greedily. He was eating the first food of most animal life in the sea. Tiny creatures eat diatoms, larger creatures eat the tiny ones, still larger animals feed on them, and so on—a chain of life from rainbow shimmers on up to Whales and beyond. In this endless food chain, Pagoo would be lucky to eat his diatoms—and not be eaten. He stared toward glassy diatom sparks as they soaked up watery sunbeams. By some strange plant magic, the diatoms were changing tasteless sunlight into tasty vegetable jelly inside themselves. But this great wonder of sunlight changing to food before his very eyes did not bother Pagoo. He didn't have to think about it. He just kept eating.

Once he started eating, Pagoo found that this ocean was one huge kettle of food. Besides crisp diatom vegetables, this kettle held soft plant jellies, or algae (*al*-jy). Wonderful algae seaweed salads came with meat floating by from the feasts of fishes. Waves churned all food into bits so small that the water itself became a sort of soup. Being sea water, of course the soup was salted exactly right. Pagoo could lie in soup and eat it too, so he was happy.

9

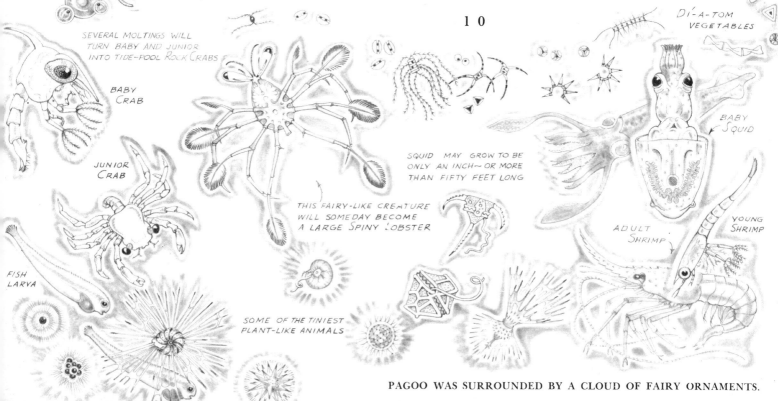

THIS JELLYFISH BECOMES ITS OWN FOOD TRAP

SOME ANIMALS CAN LIGHT-UP AT NIGHT

YOUNG BARNACLE

CO-PE-POD AN "INSECT OF THE SEA"

"SEA GOOSEBERRY" A COMB JELLYFISH CATCHES ITS FOOD

COPEPOD

ME-DU-SA JELLYFISH

MANY KINDS OF EGGS

Others besides Pagoo were eating this soup-of-the-sea. He was alone a few moments before, now he had neighbors again—the same kinds of creatures that the Shadows had been gulping. Well! So there *were* other sparkly things left in the sea, after all. Ornamental little Pagoo was being surrounded by a cloud of fairy ornaments! There were diamond stars and golden suns and red, green, blue, and purple jewels that kicked, wiggled, and danced in a restless Ballet of the Sea.

Some of Pagoo's gay companions were the very young of sea animals, just as Pagoo was a Hermit Crab in its first stages of growing. A young Spiny Lobster near Pagoo seemed made of feathers and beads. Jellyfish flashed their clearest crystal, Crabs were spun glass, a baby Squid floated by like a bulb of shining silver.

This mixed crowd with its ocean pastures of diatoms made up the restless, drifting "plankton." Plankton means "wandering," and many of the tiny animals would always drift with the diatom plants near the surface of the sea.

Other plankton creatures would grow to be larger and stronger swimmers ranging far out in the vast ocean. But many of the very young were only waiting—crowding along the sea's wrinkled ceiling till time came to drop to the ocean floor and be grown up. Pagoo, as part of this plankton crowd, awaited his turn to drop below. Meanwhile he would eat, and wander with the waves.

1 0

SEVERAL MOLTINGS WILL TURN BABY AND JUNIOR INTO TIDE-POOL ROCK CRABS

BABY CRAB

JUNIOR CRAB

FISH LARVA

SOME OF THE TINIEST PLANT-LIKE ANIMALS

THIS FAIRY-LIKE CREATURE WILL SOMEDAY BECOME A LARGE SPINY LOBSTER

SQUID MAY GROW TO BE ONLY AN INCH—OR MORE THAN FIFTY FEET LONG

DI-A-TOM VEGETABLES

BABY SQUID

ADULT SHRIMP

YOUNG SHRIMP

PAGOO WAS SURROUNDED BY A CLOUD OF FAIRY ORNAMENTS.

2. SHIFTING TIDES AND CHANGING HIDES

PAGURUS knew little about his sea, though Old Instinct tried to tell him. "It's big, son," he said. Big? To Pagoo there was no *bigness* to it—wasn't it the whole world? And on some nights there were fireworks—the whole world burning with weird, cold flames. Such displays usually began with animals small as pinheads. When disturbed by sudden water movements, their bodies took on a strangely luminous glow. Then insect-sized Copepods (co-pe-pods) caught the urge and twinkled, and other creatures after them, glow on glow, with big Jellyfish lighting up at last like pale round moons. The ghostly fire would spread and build until the sea shimmered with brightness, and huge waves fairly blazed. From this blaze a few cold sparks might tangle in Pagoo's fuzzy places. There the fairy lights would spangle Pagoo, the crystal ornament—a most natural thing in this most wonderful world. But as to a certain push-pull of water, not wind, not wave—"Tides!" said Old Pal. "It's only the tides."

For six long hours a "flood tide" slowly bulges out of the sea and creeps upon the land. Flood tide crowds wide beaches into narrow strips, and fills lagoons until boats can float and sail. Then for six hours more the "ebb tide" runs floodwaters back to sea again. Lagoons drain away until anchored boats settle down on tide flats and sit there, smack-dab in the mud! Sandy beaches spread wider, their rocks break the surface and seem to rise like monsters rearing, pools are left along shore to gleam like little lakes. Yet these puddles hold no fresh lake water. When you taste it, this water is very salty. The saltiness grows more bitter as the hot sun dries and shrinks the puddles. These "tide pools" may be as small as a bowl or as big as duckponds. But once the tide has ebbed away, it begins to return. It floods back to the tide pools and the small animals stranded there. The tidal ebb and flow never ends.

Already several days old, Pagoo never had been driven ashore— his plankton crowd had somehow held to the open sea. But on one

PINHEAD - SIZED CREATURES— NOC-TI-LU-CA ("NIGHT - SHINE") USUALLY CAUSE THE LUMINOUS GLOW KNOWN AS "SEA FIRE"

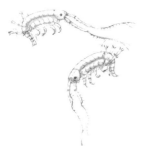

PAGOO FOUND THE TINIEST OF WATER FLEAS

1 2

SOME BEACH HOPPERS ARE INCH-LONG WHOPPERS

blue-black night when all the world was flaming with sea fire, wave, wind, and tide almost killed Pagoo. At high tide, a strong wind pushed the fire-waves into billows, rolled billions of plankton creatures into them, and charged toward land. On the crest of flood tide, Pagoo and his glowing neighbors met the coast.

Tons of tiny animals were caught up in surging spray and hurled higher than a house. Splattered with foam against the rocky cliffs, thousands of them stuck and glowed there dimly. Dry air soon put out their little fires, and they flaked away and vanished on the whirling wind. Millions of others were rolled forward, tossed and slapped upon the sandy beach. When water drained from them they flopped across great boulders of sand grains, flickered faintly, and slid off; they died in the canyons between the boulders before the next waves came. Next morning after the ebb tide, Sand Hoppers ate them. Out from the sand with a skip and a dizzy jump these Sand Fleas leaped to feast on the pale, dead plankton animals.

Pagoo was not eaten, he did not dry out. But Old Instinct had kept muttering, "Close. . . . Mighty close. . . . Too close, that time!" as Pagoo washed hard against the cliffs. Yet water formed slick cushions under him, and slid him down the rocks. Time and again he was dumped on the beach, but water swirled him, slid him back down the sloping sand to his sea again.

Pagoo was safe, though he almost had died of "wave shock." But wasn't he the son of two-fisted, fight-loving Hermit Crabs? Well, he was supposed to be, but at this stage even his own parents would not have known him. Pagoo was not two-fisted. He had no claws at all, not even legs—nothing but feelers and fuzzy things sticking out. As yet he was only a *promise* of becoming a Hermit Crab, as a caterpillar is a promise of a butterfly. But Old Pal was right there: "Sure, you are just a mite afloat on the sea, but, buck up! You are a promise. Your billions of ancestors have handed down your toughness. You can't be knocked out too easily."

MOLTING
WAS A LOT OF TROUBLE—

PAGOO BENT DOUBLE

HE LASHED
HIS TAIL

HE WRIGGLED

Yes, life in this nice salty sea could be dangerous, but Old Pal advised him, "Eat, son. Bring up your weight. Eat plenty of meat. Go chase that Water Flea." So Pagoo hunted wiggly game among the plankton, game that could be seen even by you, if you squinted. Of course the wiggly things he chased were at least as small as himself. He had found that most creatures *bigger* than he was tried to feast on *him*. In this game of run-for-your-life, you could easily be a goner!

"Keep on growing, son," urged Old Pal. You wouldn't have noticed much growth but Pagoo knew he was bigger. As though outgrowing his clothes, he felt overstuffed. "And that's dangerous," said Instinct. "Something will catch you—you're too slow. What will happen next? Why, you'll just naturally bust wide open!" And Pagoo did.

If the skin of Pagoo had been rubbery-soft like worm-skin, it could have stretched as he grew. But Pagoo's skin was not soft. It was a tough, plastic crust, for he was a Crustacean (krus-*tay*-shan) . Because Crustaceans such as Shrimps, Crawfish, Crabs, and Lobsters have crusty skins, they must "molt" to grow larger. They must burst their coverings and crawl out of them. Crustaceans molt and come out larger, soft, and wrinkled. Soon they fill out and form crusty coatings again. This happens time after time as they grow.

Pagoo's brittle armor burst open across his back. He bent double, lashed his tail, wriggled and bucked to pull all those pesky points and joints out of their plastic prisons. This molting was almost as much trouble as being hatched all over again, but at last he had shed his old skin. It drifted off in the sea like a moth's tiny wings on a breeze, and Pagoo was left soft and new all over. It felt good to be free, to stretch out and expand—and suddenly he was hungrier than ever. It was easier to bring food near his mouth parts now, for he had an extra pair of fuzzy new oars with which to stir the sea-soup.

1 4

HE BUCKED—

AT LAST HE WAS FREE
FROM HIS OLD SKIN

PAGOO STRETCHED
AND FELT NEW ALL OVER

TIDE POOLS MAY BE SMALL AS A BOWL OR BIG AS A DUCKPOND.

3. PAGOO *IS* A HERMIT CRAB!

IN THE DAYS that followed, baby Pagurus molted again and again. He ate, grew stuffed, kicked off his armor, and came out a *little* bigger each time, and with a few more improvements. He still didn't look like a Hermit Crab. He rode the wild waters away from the coast and its tide pools, and so he never had seen his grown-up relations.

At this time Pagoo was an in-between. If his part of the ocean had been dipped up in a bottle top, you might have seen him swimming around in it as a hazy blur. Under a microscope his green-glass eyes would glisten as though with intelligence, his glossy body would sparkle. Feathery things along his sides would flutter like oars being rowed, though the oars would be much too stubby, and their strokes too rapid. A slender tailpiece bending under, snapping up in a jerky motion might send him after food for his mouth parts to catch. If a lowly Water Flea had been dipped up with Pagoo, he would have barged after it, even across his whole bottle-top sea! For Old Pal had urged, "Keep growing!"

Meanwhile, among Pagoo's plankton neighbors a vast parachute drop had been going on. Many who had managed to stay alive in the bumpy upper regions came settling down. They had floated aloft as helpless youngsters. Now one by one they dropped below to a more settled life along sea bottom. They might die by the billions, but billions would live and keep going on in the ancient ways of the sea.

One day, after another hard molting, a new Pagoo popped out of his skin. He wasn't the same old baby in a larger size; he was a new model, *different!* The eyes that had hugged his head now bugged right out on stalks. Like searchlights, they could swing separately and see two ways at once. Very useful for living in an ocean. Feathery fronds still helped steer food to his mouth but Pagoo now had *jointed limbs!* Five to a side there were, long and short—ten altogether. The two front

1 6

AT THIS STAGE PAGOO LOOKED QUITE LIKE A YOUNG CRAWFISH

YOUNG PAGOO

ones moved like arms—why, Pagoo looked like a tiny Crawfish, complete with handy *claws!* So he *would* be able to box his way in the world, after all. And along with these boxing-claws went a better helmet and armor for his upper body. The lower half of him was a strong abdomen ending in a tail-paddle. One slap of that paddle could send Pagoo scooting like a Lobster.

But Crawfish and Lobsters are not Crabs. Even Pagoo would never become a true Crab. True Crabs are usually blunt at the rear, whereas Pagurus was to be an Anomuran (an-o-*mu*-ran), meaning "with an unusual tail." Pagoo did have a tail, but as yet it didn't look too unusual. (Old Pal seemed to chuckle, "It will change, boy, it sure will!")

Though related to Crawfish, Lobsters, and Crabs, he would be none of them. Yet certainly nobody of the family would object to his being called a Hermit *Crab!* Being a hermit means one who lives alone. Well, Old Instinct lived with Pagoo, but only as the wisest part of him.

Baby Pagurus was quite a boy now, with his legs, long feelers, and claws matched and even, one side like the other. After all the bother of shucking himself every so often, this lad had come out with a well-balanced body. It seemed a safe bet that Pagoo would turn into something important, with the grand look of importance you often see on a City Alderman—or on a Lobster. This boy did have promise. But Old Pal whispered, "Watch it, son. You're not there yet."

Then it happened—Pagoo molted again! And now, after all, he *was* an *anomuran!* He had kept most of his abdomen, but it was so very "unusual" as to be downright peculiar.

Poor Pagoo had come from that round of shedding his crust as though he had lost the fight entirely. It seemed that the whole world must have rolled over Pagoo, leaving him lopsided. His eyes still goggled on their stalks, he still had two good walking legs on either side of him, he had kept his claws (though the left one did seem a bit small for the likes of Pagoo). Yet, without doubt, poor little Pagoo had been changed!

PAGOO'S NEW REAR END
LOOKED DOWNRIGHT PECULIAR

The saddest change appeared at Pagoo's rear end. No longer did his bottom half look important, like that of a City Alderman or a Lobster. His trim, well-balanced abdomen had been wrenched to the right, and there it hung, slightly swollen-looking, like a crooked finger which has been stepped on. And his powerful tail-paddle? What was left of that was a bare thing like a rubber corkscrew. In fact, the whole of Pagoo's lower body had a rubbery look, because its coating was soft, not hard like the armor on his upper half. With a rear so naked, so tender, so altogether pitiful in appearance—surely *this* was not to be a fighting Hermit Crab!

"Yep, Pagoo, you're a Hermit Crab," said Old Pal. "Of course there'll be a few slight alterations here and there, but nothing much. Just keep on molting and growing."

In general, Pagoo looked like all Hermit Crabs since that tribe began—like all his close cousins in the swinging, surging, wave-tossed seas of the world. Hermits in warm seas or cold seas, Hermits on the edges of strange lands all over the globe—all of them had the twisted look of the Hermit Family, all of them had gone through the mill like Pagoo. He had come from an egg no larger than a pencil dot. He still was smaller than the eraser at the other end of the pencil, but now he was a Hermit Crab boy, not a baby.

No longer would he be pushed around at the surface by restless waves. Pagoo drifted down through nets of sunlight toward a tide-pool floor. Old Instinct was there to help him find that rocky shore with all its shallow, sandy places.

Though now he was a young boy-Hermit, Pagoo did not feel very important. Somehow he felt unprotected, not quite secure, and the unprotected feeling, he was certain, crept over him from the rear. Surely something was missing back there—his tail was not complete— he needed a—

"Scoot!" hissed Instinct. "Go find some sort of cover for that bare and tender behind!"

1 8

4. AT THE RINGSIDE

PAGURUS was worried. For weeks he had been drifting near the surface of the sea; now he walked on the bottom. He had settled down through the water when a wave had come ashore. He blundered along the floor of a tide pool in a fearful hurry. With one eye cocked at the watery shadows, the other aimed at another wave rolling above, he scuttled under a hill of rock the size of a duck egg. Somewhere nearby, waves were pounding the rocky coast.

It was not the coast that worried Pagoo. He had long forgotten his horrible bout with the tide, the surf, and the shore. He was a shore creature now, and the push-and-pull tides would be his friends. For hours he would live under several feet of salt water, while waves rolled out of the old gray ocean to pass over him and crash on the rocks beyond. For other hours he would have a quiet, shallow, sun-warmed pool to play in. Yet it was not the changing six-hour shifts, nor the shallow-deep-shallow tidal rhythm that bothered him. Pagoo was simply nervous about his rubbery rear, so helpless and exposed. He backed farther under the stone to hide himself.

As Pagoo pressed back, a Sea Worm wriggled under his corkscrew tail. Pagoo's jump was automatic, almost as high as a hotcake is thick. Old Pal was yelling, "Find another hiding place!" So Pagoo, just a dark little dot with legs all spraddled, dashed out from under the stone. As he scurried, his toes touched sand, and he heard, "Dig in!" So he squirmed backward, leaving only his eyes and feelers sticking out.

Pagoo was breathing heavily. A current of water swished over his gills under his armor, giving him new breath. Oxygen filtered out of the water like an unseen fog, passed through his gills, and soaked into his blood. Pagoo always would need oxygen. There were Hermit cousins he never had met who could take oxygen from the air itself, and so could live on the dry beach or in water, either way. Pagoo could too—for a short time. But unless his stranded pool grew stale and much too salty, he would prefer taking his oxygen from sparkling, churning sea water.

Between his two long feelers, other feathery feelers were clawing and whipping the water, setting food-flecks to jigging before his eyes. Pagoo was again reminded that he lived in a kettle of excellent soup, which sometimes thickened into a regular stew. He was still small enough to enjoy the soup, and he raked tiny particles into his mouth. There were diatom and algae vegetables, as always, and animals too small for you to see. Among torn shreds of seaweed he found meatballs floating in from some far-off meal. Pagoo was eating well, but still he was feeding as he had fed when he was a baby at the surface! Now that he was a Hermit Crab youngster on sea bottom, wasn't there some *new* way of eating?

PAGOO'S NEW CLAWS COULD PINCH

He heaved himself up and plopped his new claws on the sand. Were these things good only to fold down and flop under his body when he walked? These two new gadgets could open and shut. They could pinch! He stared at them, hearing, "Try 'em, son! They're mighty handy tools!" And all of a sudden Pagoo was busy as a sailor who has just learned how to handle chopsticks!

Pagoo laid a claw on top of a pebble, opened it, closed it, and pointed it at his mouth. To you the pebble might have looked smooth in the water, but it was all covered with algae growth. Pagoo had known algae since babyhood, in fine, floating diatom sizes. Down here it came also in filmy coatings, or fuzzy like velvet, or soft and deep as moss. In fact, the real seaweeds—from tender, leafy "sea-lettuce" up to tough kelp plants a hundred feet long—were all algae. But Pagoo was not interested in big seaweed algae; he preferred to hunt food in the fuzzy algae on the pebble. His claws opened and shut and he ate greedily, pleased with his new scissor-pincher-plucker tools.

Then a couple of somethings whirled from nowhere and plopped near Pagoo. They flopped around! Pagoo shrank back, fearing a blow,

2 1

but nothing happened Mud clouds spurted and drifted off in watery haze, and he wasn't hurt—he was frightened. He tried backing farther under the sand, but his tender tail struck solid rock below.

Pagoo kept still except for his quivering feelers and his jerking eyes. He heard Old Instinct, as though tuned in from a vast distance and from an ancient time: "Those two strangers standing before you —they're HERMIT CRABS!"

They were big fellows, each of them twelve times the size of small Pagoo. How big is that in terms of people? Well, if you are a six-foot man (which is doubtful), then a building twelve times your height would be about seven stories tall. So, compared to tiny Pagurus. those two Hermits were as big as barns!

Pagoo did not go racing out to his new-found relatives, waving a welcome. He was as still as stone. The two big bruisers stood glaring at each other, legs wide, arms out, gloves ready. As though Pagoo had watched boxing bouts a million years back in his memory, there seemed nothing strange in all this, nor in the fighters' costumes. With helmeted heads and shoulders forward, their tender tails were curled inside rounded boxing trunks. These were old Snail Shells, over an inch wide. Shell-layers worn off by surf had left them many-colored.

Now the fighters side-stepped, dragging their shells along, *rumpety-bump*. They darted out on pointed toes, drew back weaving. What well-matched specimens of the water arena! Such graceful sparring!

Now they rush together, gloves swinging, they jab and jab again, they counter with swift crosses, their uppercuts start low, from the very bottom of the sea, now they go into a clinch. . . .

Sand and mud swirled like cigar smoke over the whole arena. As Pagoo stared goggle-eyed at the ringside, both boxers slammed into him. Their heavy shells rolled over him, banged his feelers and claws, and hammered his tender body hidden under the sand.

2 2

PAGOO STARED GOGGLE-EYED AT THE RINGSIDE.

5. A RIDE AND A FALL FAR, FAR FROM HOME

PAGOO was only a tiny mite, there in the tide pool, but he was angry through the entire length of him. No matter how big those two Hermit boxers were, they just couldn't go bashing his feelers and face with those heavy shell tails! He'd show 'em!

Pagoo's mad leap from his sand pit barely rolled six grains of sand from his own tail. As a leap, it was a flop! This was not like the old days at the surface, when a snap of his gleaming tail could spring him forward. Though still under water he was a landlubber now, and his stubby tail had no more spring to it than a coil of mud. It was plain that where he wanted to go, he must walk. So he walked.

Pagoo walked right over, grabbed one of those roughnecks by the wrinkled seat of his fighting trunks, and climbed the fat bulge of the shell clear to the top. He teetered on the edge of the opening and stared down. Far below him the battler's helmeted head and shoulders leaned from the shell. It was too far away for a hit, yet Pagoo swung. A *left* with his small glove! A sweeping *right,* which almost upset him. His childish blows just could not connect, he was merely fanning the water. Then the big boys started their next round. The fight broke out again right under Pagoo, and the confusion blew his anger into the sea. But in his mind (if Pagoo *had* a mind) were the shouts of Old Pal: "Hang on, boy! HANG ON!"

Little Pagoo seemed to be the referee of this fight, this whirling merry-go-round. From his high perch on the shell—right on top of things, as you might say—he was in a perfect position to learn pointers on Hermit boxing. However, Pagoo soon was much too busy to see a thing. What mind he had went blank. The boxers beneath him took off over mountains of Mussel Shells, into clusters of Barnacles, through jungles of stranded kelp. The fighters staggered right into the center of a Sea Anemone (a-*nem*-o-nee). Pagoo held on for dear life and was

2 4

hauled out before the Anemone's tentacles clutched the three of them.

Oh, Pagoo met that tide pool fore, aft, and amidships—but he was too fagged and fogged to notice details. Sometimes on top, sometimes under, his rubbery rear couldn't take the walloping. He was *so* tired. He *had* to let go and slide off.

Pagoo had dismounted in rugged country. He sprawled on his back in a canyon, with cliffs and ridges of Mussel Shells on either side. A moment ago he had galloped over these very ridges. Now he didn't know them. When you're down in the gullies, the world looks different from the beautiful way it looks when you're riding high.

Pagoo rolled himself over. His right claw jerked outward and clicked against a Mussel. Getting to his feet, he whisked both feelers over the rounded surface of the shell. SHELL? Old Instinct whispered, "Sure, son, you ought to know that stuff is *shell*. And what you need right now is a *shell* to sit in. You're sort of naked back there. Nature has changed your shape to fit in a shell. So, *go find* one!"

Yes, a shell was what Pagoo wanted now, more than anything else in the whole world of water! Pagoo needed a shell to sit in like those fat, round trunks the two fighters wore. But not so large. Pagoo needed a small shell. This Mussel thing in front of him was a whopper. And where was the way in? He reared back and swung both eye-stalks up —and up. Why, this was two shells, clamped together!

Pagoo did not know that the soft Mussel animal inside was a Mollusk (*moll*-usk), nor that its two shells made it a bivalve (*bi*-valve), and he didn't much care. The double-shelled Mussel towered up from the canyon many times taller than little Pagoo was long. The Mussel hugged its doors so tightly together, Pagoo just couldn't get in!

He skittered up the lumpy valley, both eyes wagging, his feelers tapping and poking around corners. He found no hole that would stay open. Some Mussels spread their shell-doors slightly, like a book opened only a little, to feed on sea-soup. But Pagoo's softest feeler-tap snapped those book-doors shut! Pagoo had almost lost his feelers.

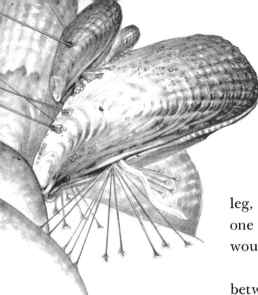

THE MUSSEL LAYS ITS STRONG
PLASTIC ANCHOR THREADS WITH
A SLENDER GROOVED FOOT

Pagoo was lucky to be a Crustacean. If he had lost a feeler, a leg, or even a claw, he would not have been disabled forever. A new one would grow, bulging under his crust. When he molted again it would unfold, ready for use.

Since Pagoo could not climb into a Mussel, he decided to hide between two of them, but there wasn't much chance. These mountain peaks were too close together. Well then, he'd tunnel under somewhere! But he couldn't even get started. He was stopped by nets of cords like jungle roots, horny things thick as silk thread. All these byssus (*bi*-sus) threads fastened each Mussel to its rocky base, roped Mussel to Mussel, sewed up the spaces between. Each Mussel had spun its own cables to moor it fast against the violent waves and tides. Pagoo saw one Mussel laying a new byssus mooring line.

The Mussel's book-doors spread wide enough for a slender "foot" to stretch out. More like a finger than a foot, it reached until it pressed on the rock several inches away. A sticky fluid, from a gland inside the Mussel's body, ran down a groove in the foot like soft taffy sliding down a trough. In a couple of minutes the taffy had hardened in the water, to become a plastic byssus thread tightly strung.

Pagoo moved a feeler ever so little, yet the startled Mussel hauled up its foot and snapped its book-doors shut. Well, no matter. Pagoo didn't want a two-shell, bivalve home. He seemed to want a one-shell, univalve (*u*-ni-valve) house. Yes, and it should be small—his size— and empty, of course. He would search, and find one right away. He promptly stepped on his gloves, tripped over the new cable, and went sprawling.

Once more tired little Pagoo lay on his back in the canyon, staring up at the Mussel peaks. They towered above him, ridge after ridge, growing pale in the watery distance beyond the tide pool, toward the open sea.

2 6

6. A STARFISH, AND A FEW BARNACLES

As PAGOO lay in the Mussel canyon, tiny creatures came crawling from cracks and crannies. The rowdy Hermit boxers had sent them zipping into holes, and Pagoo's restless house-hunting had kept them there. But, *this* naked little Hermit was really harmless!

How could so many of them live among Mussel mooring lines where even tiny Pagoo couldn't crowd in? Crabs smaller than young Pagoo eyed him from the matted growth. All sorts of wiggly Worms and jointed beings came helter-skelter on fluttering fringes of legs. "Flatworms" with no legs at all flowed past Pagoo like thin blobs of molasses dribbling off a spoon. Pagoo rolled to his feet, found a long, fat Mussel leaning out from the big rock like a springboard, walked the bulging shell to its end, and peered over.

This rocky place, this "Mussel Ridge," sloped down and down before fading into watery dimness. Crouched like a polka dot with legs, Pagoo felt this ten-foot drop was just *too* deep. As a floating baby he had drifted over mile-deep places, but of course he couldn't remember. Now he was jittery. Somehow he wouldn't want to find a shell home way down there! Strange shapes moved in this "Deep Hole." Even now a something was climbing the rock, gliding ever so slowly up from the deep shadows—a purple Starfish with five arms. One arm began to lift its tip, pointing toward Pagoo, and Old Pal said, "He's too slow to catch you—" But Pagoo didn't wait for more. He scuttled backward down the springboard, stumbled over its byssus anchor cords, and landed once more in a canyon. He righted himself and ran!

Skittering past more Mussels, he bumped into the bouncy stalk of a Goose Barnacle (*bar*-na-kul). This animal's top part grew bony plates like flat teeth plastered to its rubbery sides. The toothy look didn't frighten Pagoo, but—well, he saw no chance of a home in a Goose Barnacle. He walked away, keeping an eye on the Starfish.

A MUSSEL BED
IS A CROWDED PLACE

INSIDE SOME MUSSELS
A SMALL SOFT PEA CRAB
MAKES HER HOME AND
SHARES THE MUSSEL'S FOOD

2 8

FLATWORMS SEEM TO 'FLOW' OVER A ROCK—
BUT WITH EDGES RUFFLED
THEY ARE GRACEFUL SWIMMERS

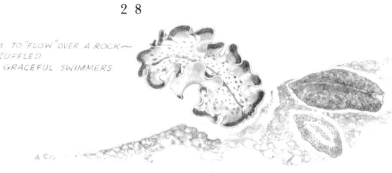

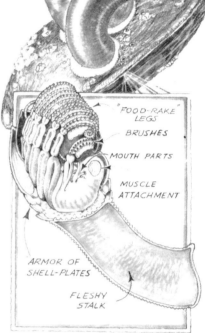

GOOSE OR
GOOSENECK BARNACLES
GROW ON LONG FLESHY STALKS

ONCE IN A WHILE
YOUNG BARNACLES
SETTLE DOWN ON ADULTS

BARNACLE
FEEDING

"FOOD-RAKE"
LEGS

BRUSHES

MOUTH PARTS

MUSCLE
ATTACHMENT

ARMOR OF
SHELL-PLATES

FLESHY
STALK

INSIDE ITS SHELL-PLATES ~ GOOSE
OR GOOSENECK BARNACLE
RESTS ON ITS BACK, LEGS CURLED UP

The Starfish glided on tube-feet like tiny soda straws. Many of them stretched, took a suction grip, and pulled the Starfish along. The purple animal reached the Mussel springboard, felt around carefully, and slowly straddled the tight crack where the book-doors met. Three of its arms fastened their tube-feet to one shell, the last two arms clutched the other shell. So this thing was after Mussels, *not* Pagoo!

Pagoo left the Goose Barnacles with their rubbery stalks, and came to the hard shell of a Red Barnacle stuck tight to the rock. This animal's inch-high home looked like an Indian tepee stretching high above Pagoo. Nearby were other kinds of Acorn Barnacles. But the Red Barnacles made an Indian village complete with a haze that looked something like smoke swirling from the tepee tops.

"Don't let that hazy swirl fool you," said Old Pal. "It's just *legs*. You see, Barnacles are your own distant relatives—that is, they are all Crustaceans. Each Barnacle builds a shell house around himself. As he grows he molts, and kicks his old skin out the door of his shell. He stands on his head and rakes food down to his mouth with feathery *legs*."

Could Pagoo scare a Barnacle out of its red tepee and take over? Old Pal said, "No," but Pagoo was already climbing the shell like a farm boy on the ladder of a concrete silo. At the jagged top he peeked inside, and—well, Old Pal was right. Though it could twist a little bit inside its tepee, that Barnacle was stuck by the back of its neck to the tepee's concrete floor. How sensitive it was! It hauled down its fuzzy legs, right past Pagoo's face, snapped its double-action doors shut, and was not open to visitors.

While he was up so high, Pagoo swung both eyes again toward that Starfish. Its tube-feet, gripping the Mussel's doors, were holding, pulling. Great strain bulged the purple arms, swelling the Starfish like a fantastic tent above the shellfish. Its pulling power could lift a hundred pounds, but the hidden muscles of the Mussel held fast. No crack appeared between those doors—as yet. But the Star's strength

"PINK" BARNACLES
MAKE TALL SHELLS WHEN CROWDED

"RED" OR ROCK
BARNACLES

ACORN-TYPE   BARNACLES   HAVE   SHELLS   OF   MANY   SHAPES

UNCROWDED   "PINK"
BARNACLES

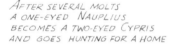

ALL KINDS OF BARNACLE BABIES
WANDER WITH THE PLANKTON

NAU´-PLI-US
STAGE

CY´-PRIS STAGE

AFTER SEVERAL MOLTS
A ONE-EYED NAUPLIUS
BECOMES A TWO-EYED CYPRIS
AND GOES HUNTING FOR A HOME

AT LAST A CYPRIS BECOMES
A TRUE YOUNG BARNACLE.
SETTLED SECURELY IN SOME
SHELTERED PLACE, IT WILL GROW.

could outlast shellfish strength. Hour after hour it could cling there, two bulging arms steadily tugging at one door, three arms hauling and straining at the other. . . .

Pagoo climbed down from his Barnacle perch. So Barnacles were relatives? Crusty old things, sticktights, never going places like Pagoo. As though disgusted, Pagoo kicked at a tepee.

He did not remember his surface days, and millions of Barnacle babies among the plankton. Like Pagoo, they passed through the first two stages of Crustaceans, and stopped there. They didn't go on to change into Shrimps, Lobsters, or Crabs. They dropped toward sea bottom, becoming what they were supposed to be all the time—Barnacles. Making mortar from lime in the water, they cemented themselves to rocks, wood, shells, or anything handy, even other Barnacles. They built hard shells, stuck up jointed legs, and kicked their food down.

Of course Pagoo was restless, hunting a shell—unlike feather-footed Barnacles, he could use *his* legs for traveling! But he had rubbed feelers with Barnacle babies who would travel where he could never go. Settled on the backs of Sea Turtles, some kinds would live in tropic waters. Whales would carry other kinds to Arctic or Antarctic seas. Still others, hugging wooden boat hulls and steel ship bottoms, would prowl the world's oceans, living well on sea-soup all the way. These crusty boat travelers never would understand that the masses of their stony houses add tons of weight to ships, dragging down their speed. Peaceful Barnacle colonies cause much anger among sea captains. It costs a lot to scrape a ship's bottom, "foul" with Barnacles, when it finally drags into home port.

Pagoo had his eyes on a heap of Pink Barnacles built up like a fairy castle. At the very top a mere button of one of them stuck to the one below it. Wasn't that about the size for Pagoo? From where he stood on Mussel Ridge, it looked vacant, empty, and he climbed toward it. Meanwhile the Starfish was winning its tug of war with the Mussel, and the hard book-doors were slowly opening. . . .

3 0

AS A BARNACLE
MOLTS TO GROW,
IT ALSO ENLARGES
ITS SHELL

BARNACLES STRAIN THEIR SEA-SOUP
WITH LEGS LIKE A FEATHERED RAKE.
SHORTER BRUSHES SORT OUT TIDBITS.

O-PER´-CU-LUM
DOOR CLOSED
BY MUSCLE

MOUTH

SHELL SECTION

WHEN THE TIDE IS OUT ALL BARNACLES WAIT,
CURLED FEET-UP, BENEATH ARMORED DOORS

PAGOO SWUNG BOTH EYES
TOWARD THAT BIG STAR.

7. ROOM AND BOARD, TRAVEL INCLUDED

PAGOO climbed the towers of Pink Barnacles. The top of the highest tower held a very small button of a Barnacle Shell. Pagoo finally reached this tiny penthouse. He tapped it with his feelers, felt all around inside, and found it—EMPTY! He hopped right in.

The hollow button would do for Pagoo! It wasn't *exactly* right, of course, because his rear had grown curved for coiling into *Snail Shells*. This empty Barnacle house was spread out at the bottom. It left spaces where currents of cold water could flow in around his bare tail. Pagoo didn't complain. His first home, it was; solid cement, too! No danger could come from behind. As for protection up front, he seemed to get advice from Old Instinct: "Put 'em up, boy! Cover yourself!" So Pagoo ducked behind his gloves and, sure enough, they made a door to his shelter. Now just let anything try to get in! In the shadows of his penthouse, exhausted Pagoo relaxed quietly. Though both eyes always would be open, he was having a Hermit Crab sleep.

While Pagoo snoozed, the purple Starfish began eating his shellfish meal. How? He had no mouth like yours, no tongue nor teeth, but he did have a very remarkable stomach. And with this remarkable stomach, a Starfish is quite direct about his eating.

Just as your meat is sometimes made more tender by soaking it in tenderizing liquid, a Starfish has his own special solution to tenderize Mussel meat. While his Mussel steaks become very tender, the Star spreads out his stomach like a frilled napkin. Draping it over the food in the double-shell serving tray, he absorbs the dainties right through it, with no smacking of lips, no grinding of molars, no vulgar gulping. When he has finished, little is left but two clean pearly plates to show that a bright Star has dined at this table. . . .

Pagoo sprang awake from his snooze to find his water world changing! Already new currents swirled into his tide pool. Where low-tide water had been calm, growing warm in the sun, stale and bitter with salt, this liquid was different. Cold, clear, it was frothy new water direct from the open sea. Sloshing around Pagoo's new home, it had dashed him out of his trance. He promptly dropped his two-glove door, leaned from his Barnacle penthouse, and gazed about. Flood tide was nothing new to Pagoo, but for the first time he had a grandstand seat from which to watch it come.

Pagoo felt a rumble of vibrations, which began and stopped far away. The rumblings came again and again, stopping beyond the rock of the Mussels and the deep hole beside it. Little by little the rolling waves came closer, did *not* stop at Deep Hole or Mussel Ridge, rushed right over Pagoo, and crashed against cliffs. Wave suction tugged at him; bubbles trailed down from the surface to burst in his face.

He was not afraid. This new water brought new food, and Pagoo's mouth parts were fairly galloping. He hadn't *known* such hunger! Fresh diatom and algae vegetables, a tasty flake or two of Herring. And there went a Water Flea, tearing past with a teasing wiggle—whoops, Pagoo missed! Below him the Barnacle hatches had popped open, the plumes of their legs were up and flying like banners waving from castle towers. Pagoo breathed deeply. Oh, such wonderful, fresh oxygen! Such fizzing, tickling bubbles!

Looking down, he saw that the tide pool had come to life. Even the sunlight was merrier—a million fragments of light went streaming along the tide-pool floor. From cracks and holes came mobs of creatures. Dots with legs slithered from weeds, larger dots joined them, feet and feelers boiled up from nowhere, untangling into countless small animals. Little fishes darted by. A dizziness of relief that the waters were no longer stale, a hunger craziness at finding fresh foods, a madness of glee seemed to swell, wave after wave, across the old tide pool. Even Pagoo grew dizzy with it all—and little wonder, for his very *foundations* were shifting! His shelter lurched and swayed. The penthouse, with Pagoo inside it, was traveling!

Pagoo's Barnacle towers had grown on a two-inch Smooth-Turban Shell, made by a Snail, and inside that shell lived a fat lady Hermit. What with Pagoo lodged in her attic, she was his landlady, though she had been sleeping when he took the room and Pagoo hadn't known that she was living down below. She wobbled quite a bit when she walked, but, of course, she was carrying an apartment building. Now she squatted under her Traveling Towers.

Pagoo's Landlady knew a pert little fish from around the corner. He often brought goodies to her. He himself only picked at his food, and seemed to be eating nothing at all, but that was because of his size. He was three inches long, but his mouth was too tiny for really good bites. Yet every so often he grew very hungry for a good meat dinner. He was clever at finding chunks of meat, but they usually were too large for him to swallow whole, so he would take the piece to the Landlady of Traveling Towers.

Now he arrived with some meat. It might have come from the Star's dinner, but from wherever it came, here it was! The little fish was gone in a flash, his food bundle left with the Landlady.

Oh, she knew what to do with it, it was her place to carve and serve. Well, at least she would carve. She whisked out her cutters and shredded that meat to a fare-thee-well. It wasn't her fault that her Barnacle roomers caught scattered crumbs, or that delicate portions were delivered by elevator (the current was working just right) to Pagoo, three and a half flights up. The small fish swished back again, not at all bashful about getting *his,* and the right size, too. Everyone was happily satisfied. But when a huge Crab tried to claw himself into the party, everyone moved.

Yes, Pagoo had been lucky in choosing his first home—a snug penthouse apartment, with free sea-food dinners included! Old Pal said, "Wait, this fancy stuff isn't for you—" but Pagoo did not listen. He leaned back in his rocking penthouse like a well-fed rajah riding off somewhere in his jeweled elephant howdah.

3 4

THE LITTLE FISH LEFT HIS BUNDLE
OF FOOD WITH THE LANDLADY.

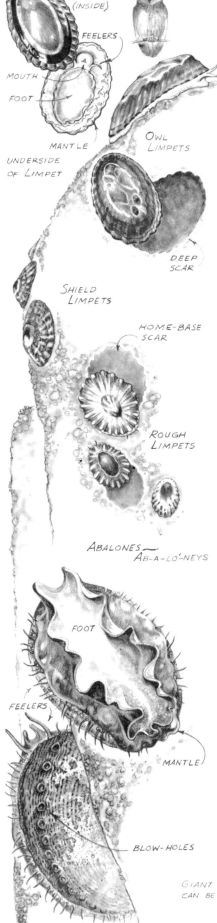

8. AROUND SNAIL COUSINS' ROCK

PAGOO's penthouse rocked and reeled as the angry Landlady waddled away from the big Crab. As for the big Crab, he knew she had been eating Mussel meat. Did she have more? Well, he'd sure find it, or he'd eat *her!* He rushed up and toppled Traveling Towers with one claw. He poked, he pried—and got nothing. All doors were locked. He scuttled away in disgust. . . .

When certain that the bandit had gone, the Landlady pried her apartments upright again. Nearby, Pagoo saw a big shell like an ear clamped to the rock. This univalve had a row of holes which spouted small currents of water. So some animal lived and breathed and fed, under that shell! Pagoo drew back as this Abalone (ab-a-*lo*-ney) began gliding away on a broad black foot. Pagoo had watched the Mussel's foot spin cables to anchor it, but this thick Abalone's foot was an anchor all in itself! It gripped with powerful suction. An Abalone is hard to pry loose when it decides to put its foot down! Now this creature slid away on the rock like a crawling Snail.

A Snail-pace is natural for an Abalone, the Snail's first cousin. This rock was an old family homestead for many Snail relatives. They stuck around all over the place. When these bumps on Snail Cousins' Rock didn't move, Pagoo went to sleep.

Most of the bumps here were Limpets (*lim*-pets), univalves like the Abalone. Some shells looked like fancy oval buttons painted with stripes and spots. Others had holes on top, like volcanoes. Most Limpets stay home during low tide. At high tide they glide over their rocks to scrape up tiny plants with a raspy tongue. They always return to home base, a neat "scar" the exact size and oval shape of the owner. No other Limpet will ever camp on that spot. Each finds its own scar and settles down—a mere bump on a rock!

Teetering up Snail Cousins' Rock, the Landlady jerked to a wobbly stop that awakened Pagoo. He watched waves bubbling far

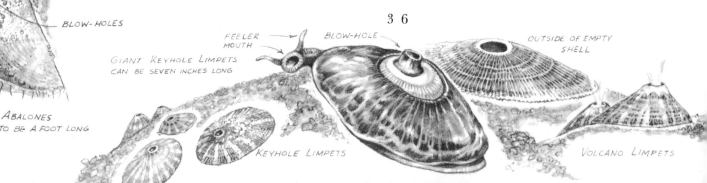

above him. He looked below at a tangle of kelp washing in, dragging
its boulder-anchor. The Landlady fumbled with this algae plant till
she found its long stem. Then she went into her waddle on this floating
highway. Pagoo was lulled into a gentle snooze once more, and again
was jerked awake. This time he bonged about in his roomy Barnacle
like a clapper in a bell!

Traveling Towers was thumping among little balloons—air floats
looking like green plums. These floats lift and hold their long kelp
plants upright in the sea, but this one was just about wrecked. The
Landlady bumped, balloon to balloon, and each bump banged Pagoo.
He felt better when she reached smooth, leaflike "blades." On a kelp
bridge arching above Snail Cousins' Rock, Traveling Towers dragged
to a stop. Carrying a full apartment building had made the Landlady
hungry. She began plucking some food.

The no-more-bumps jolted Pagoo wider awake. He popped from
his doorway and peered down. She was eating again. Good! He waited,
but not one meat particle floated up to him. So there were drawbacks
to living in Traveling Towers. Stuck way up there, he couldn't go
places on his own. He would climb down—but a fish-shadow below sent
him right back up. Glumly he batted his feelers. Nothing but common
old sea-soup again!

From time to time Pagoo swung an eye at the kelp-streamers
below. He saw several Snail relations *not* stuck to the rock. A Sea Slug
was a Snail Cousin with no shell at all. Pagoo's eyes fairly spun when
one slid past on a nearby kelp blade. This Nudibranch (*noo*-de-brangk)
was a dazzling creature, bright and frilly. This Nudibranch could
crawl or swim. A three-inch sample of fancy silk ribbon, it flowed or
fluttered along. Snails build themselves gay-colored shells. This Nudibranch spent her energy on gorgeous clothes.

Like a drowsy rabbit, a huge Snail relative nibbled kelp. Two
curled feelers like rabbit ears gave the Sea Hare its name. This smooth
sluggish animal wore no outer shell. As it breathed, wing-like ruffles

AIR-FILLED FLOATS
OF KELP

SPECIAL LIMPETS
LIVE ONLY ON
KELP STEMS

AMONG ALGAE PLANTS
KELP IS A GIANT
SEAWEED

ROOT-LIKE HOLD-FASTS
ANCHOR SEAWEED
TO A ROCK

DUNCE-CAP
LIMPETS

SIPHON

FEELERS

THE SEA HARE IS A SNAIL WITHOUT A SHELL.
IT LOOKS RATHER LIKE A RABBIT WITH RUFFLES.

3 7

MOST OF THE SNAILS AND SOME OF THEIR COUSINS
SCRAPE UP THEIR FOOD WITH A RADULA

PLAN OF A SNAIL'S RAD-U-LA

SOME PERIWINKLE SNAILS CAN
LIVE PART TIME OUT OF WATER

DOG-WHELKS LIKE MEAT —
ANY MEAT — FRESH OR NOT

OLIVE SNAILS PLOW THROUGH WET SAND
TO FIND BITS OF FOOD LEFT BY THE WAVES

TIP OF "PULLEY"

HUNDREDS OF SHARP TEETH
COVER THE STRAP-LIKE RADULA

LIPS

HARD "PULLEY"

MUSCLES

FOOD

MUSCLES ① AND ② PULL,
SNAIL SCRAPES UP FOOD.
① AND ② RELAX WHILE
③ AND ④ PULL

SNAIL'S
GENERAL PLAN

PAIR OF FEELERS
MOUTH WITH
RADULA

SHELL

MANTLE

FOOT

O-PER'-CU-LUM
(DOOR)

BLACK
TURBANS

THE TURBAN TRIBE
LIKES ALGAE SALADS

BROWN
TURBAN

SPECKLED
TURBANS

SMOOTH TURBANS

UNDERSIDE OF
COWRY SHELL

COLONIES OF TUBE SNAILS NEED NO RADULAS.
THEY SNARE FOOD WITH THEIR STICKY GILLS.

CONES

A WAVY-TOP SNAIL HAS A FANCY O-PER'-CU-LUM (DOOR)
OPERCULUM

COWRY AND CONE SNAILS HAVE NO DOORS

on its back flapped gently or folded into a spout. Though its size was amazing, Pagoo felt safe near this eyeless giant. It seemed quite defenseless. Yet it could discourage any enemy by squirting a cloud of purple fluid around. Ugh! *Very* distasteful!

No animals care to stop Sea Hares from growing, once they have started. This one might grow to a bulky sixteen pounds, and it would lay millions and millions of eggs. Luckily, many animals *do* eat the eggs of Sea Hares. Otherwise, in a few years the world's oceans would be packed as solid as a can of sardines with these soft Snail cousins.

The Snails with shells were feeding everywhere, and Pagoo heard, "Son, you've got a tail-length feeling that a Snail Shell should be your home—and you're right. Even the Landlady's Smooth-Turban Shell was made by a Snail. Now look around you at the live ones!"

Each Snail was grazing, scraping off algae growth with its radula (*rad*-u-la). This tongue moved like a strap pulled forward and back. Where the radula pressed down, sharp-edged blades like the teeth of a file rasped the algae food from rock and weed.

Pagoo saw only the *shells* of the Snails. Rounded, smooth, and shiny shells, sharply pronged and pointed shells, shells long and slender, short and fat, shells like olives, cones, and fancy buttons, spinning tops and rajah turbans. And they came in all sizes. But could he leap down, yank a Snail from its shell and take over? That wise character Instinct seemed to say, "It isn't being done. Hermits long ago found it too much trouble to pull out a living Snail. It sticks to its house like a Barnacle. But Snails finally die, and other creatures clean their shells out, spick and span. Someday you'll find heaps of empty shells."

All of a sudden Pagoo forgot about shells. Something terrible happened to Traveling Towers. The Landlady on the main floor, the five pink concrete towers crowded with Barnacles, even little Pagoo high in his penthouse—all were *swallowed!*

3 8

ABOVE SNAIL COUSIN'S ROCK,

TRAVELING TOWERS DRAGGED TO A STOP.

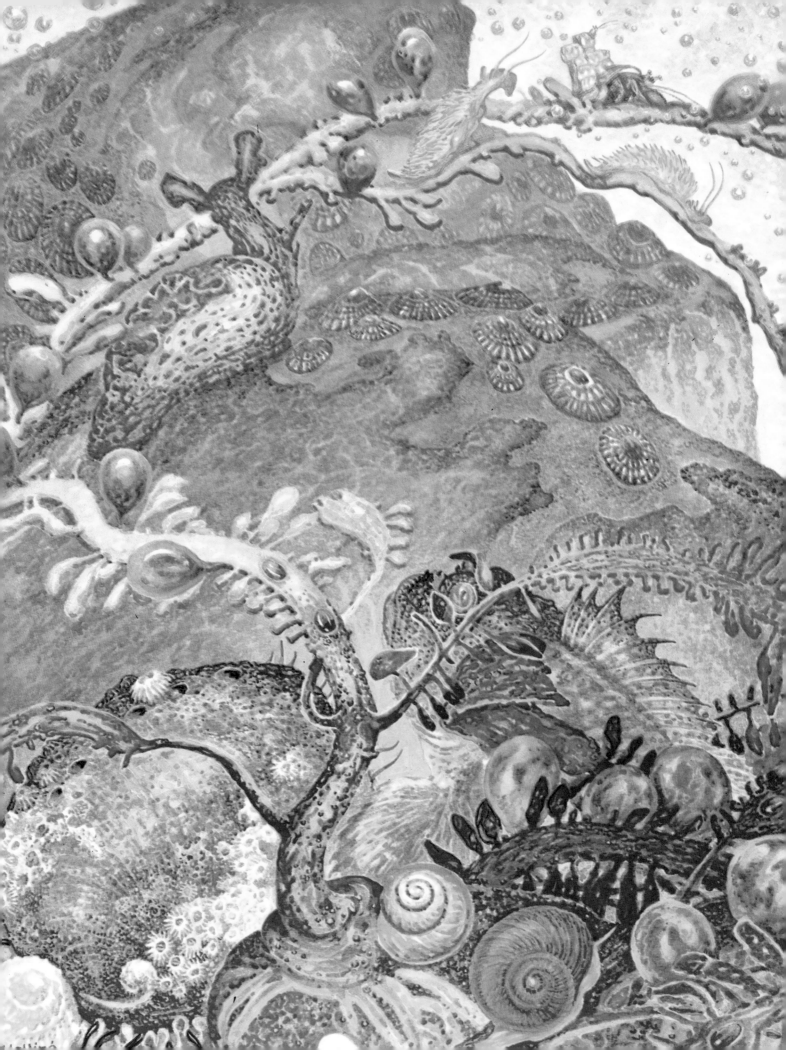

9. IN, OUT, UP WITH TRAVELING TOWERS

THE FISH who had swallowed Pagurus (along with his Landlady, five Barnacles, and seven shells of Traveling Towers), was Big Head the Sculpin. He came and went with the tides, and you just could not see him. His huge head and mottled body were spiked and fringed with floppy, mossy parts. When he lingered near rocks, or pebbly bottom, or shivering seaweed, his colors changed to fit the scenery and you could not tell which was which. If he did not move—well, he could not *be* there. But just when you thought he was *not* there, then Big Head ate you. Sculpins had been skulking around like this for a long time. A Sculpin was one of the dangers of tide-pool living. He was to be learned about and forgotten, except deep inside—with nerves all set for getaway action whenever he might appear. So, nobody worried. Many timid creatures live in the sea, and most of them have their enemies, but always enough of them survive to carry on.

Pagoo had been swallowed. Just like that. However, luck was with him: the Sculpin was not feeling well this morning. Big Head had charged a Sea Hare—and its powerful purple cloud had bounced him back like a blow in the face. He sulked in the weeds, still hungry —and then he spied Traveling Towers and the Landlady. Fresh Hermit! And fresh Barnacles, too. He would digest them all and later toss out the empty shells. He charged with mouth wide open. Ugh! What a *rough* lump! He dashed near the shore, and heaved out Traveling Towers!

Had this been a lesson to Pagoo? What lesson can be learned in the very jaws of death? Old Instinct had gone deathly silent. What was there left to say? Pagoo was confused. No part of this had been his fault. At times some misfortune gulps you down, and you learn only one small thing. Pagoo had learned to beware of such creatures as Sculpins. And maybe this one lesson was quite enough for now. . . .

The Landlady had been as confused as Pagoo. She had not seen Big Head coming, and when it was too late—well, it was too late. But the horny-headed fish had not held Traveling Towers for long. The Landlady felt peculiar vibrations as the Sculpin's front fins jerked, his tail lashed madly, carrying them on. Then, violent shudders, and all passengers suddenly were un-gulped, not far from shore.

The Landlady was galloping when she hit tide-pool bottom, and she did not stop. She would get away from where Sculpins cruised. At the very edge of the pool she backed her apartments beneath a ledge where Big Head could not come. What an awful experience! The Barnacles may have felt likewise, but they gave no sign. Everyone cleaned legs and feelers, and all hands of Traveling Towers sank into deep sleep, exhausted.

Pagoo awoke first and noticed it—no water for breathing! Old Pal yelled for OXYGEN! Pagoo poked his head out of the door—and into dry rock. Backing under the ledge, the Landlady had squeezed Pagoo's room against the cave roof—he couldn't get out! The Landlady awoke and noticed the changes. She shuddered. Was she still inside the Sculpin? No, her feet were near sea water—sea water growing stale and saltier as it dried up in a shallow shore pool at low tide. SHORE? *LOW TIDE?*

She lurched forward, half out of her shell. Her feelers waved in empty air. Traveling Towers was stranded! She *must move!*

She couldn't budge her house. Tug and strain as she might, she had done her job too well when scrambling under the rock. Traveling Towers was stuck, above water. Pagoo's penthouse was barely damp from the wash of a last low ripple. The Landlady had not known Pagoo very well, if at all, but she could feel him rattling around upstairs, banging his fists on the walls. She had a hazy idea that he wanted to get out of there. Well, so did she.

A clamor of curlews, sandpipers, and gulls told that these birds were raiding the beach for tidbits left by the tide. Curlews walking

4 1

CURLEW

SPARROW-SIZED
SANDPIPER

with stately steps, ran their down-curved beaks into holes after hidden, squirming food. Sandpipers scudded across the wet beach like sandy shadows. Gulls found Clams, and flapped and screamed with joy.

Each Clam tried to dig deeper into wet sand. Its narrow foot poked down, then swelled up into a ball. The Clam pulled its shell-covered body down to this ball-anchor. The faster it poked, balled-up, and pulled, the faster it sank in the sand. But gulls are quick, and many Clams were caught. When a Clam was dragged out, it tucked in its foot and its twin tubes for feeding and breathing, and snapped its doors. Inside muscles put on pressure, hugging the doors together.

A gull caught a Clam in its beak, flew high with it, and let go. The Clam fell, turning over and over, struck a rock and almost seemed to explode. The gull swooped after it to feed on Clam meat. Another gull soared up, dropping its Clam, not on rock, but on hard sand— and still the Clam broke open. Because of the tension of those pulling muscles, the shells of the Clam shattered inward with the blow.

Meanwhile, the Landlady of Traveling Towers was doing a desperate thing. Quick as a flash she popped from her shell, spun around, and clutched her apartment house. This way, that way she tugged with her claws. She pushed, pulled, and twisted. She was so anxious to loosen the thing that she forgot her tender unprotected rear.

The Landlady's eyes still were sharp, and she saw the gull descending. Letting everything go she backed into her shell and clapped her glove-door shut. She did it all in one movement, as though she were a toy snapped in by a rubber band.

The hungry gull teetered on slippery stones, hunched over, and peered beneath the ledge. A fat Hermit was somewhere in that barnacled lump—he had seen her himself! She was one mouthful he was going to get. He gripped the rough lump of shells with his beak and wrenched it loose. Up into the sky he flew with Traveling Towers!

4 2

GULL
WITH LANDLADY

THE LANDLADY SAW THE GULL DESCENDING.

10. HOUSES ARE SCARCE IN TIDE–POOL TOWN

THE GULL flew up and up with the barnacled lump of Traveling Towers. He opened his beak, dropped the lump, and followed it down lest another gull catch the hidden Crab when the thing burst open. Traveling Towers missed the rocks and bounced on wave-packed sand. The bird landed and straddled the lump with beak open and ready. Yet nothing had broken. No Crab appeared. He blinked foolishly and glanced at his gull neighbors, who had their eyes on him. Their clamming was over because the Clams had dug beyond their reach. The gull scooped up his bumpy lump for another try.

This time he soared higher in wider spirals. Perhaps the audience watching below made him nervous, because on this bombing-run he missed his rock target and hit the water. He missed rocks *and* sand, and Traveling Towers plopped into two feet of tide pool. Looking very foolish, the bird flapped off down the beach, followed by squawks and shrieks which sounded like gull laughter.

Pagoo felt woozy with it all. He also was disgusted with life in Traveling Towers. At first it had been so wonderful—a meat dinner, travel, sightseeing—and all of it free, without any work from him. But sightseeing inside a Sculpin had not been nice. And he hadn't liked drying out at ebb tide, nor choking for want of oxygen, nor flapping into the sky to choke on too much of the stuff! Down, down he had fallen. Up again, down again. That water was *hard* when he hit from the highdive! Still, it was good old sea water. He lay, soaking it in. His gills still worked, his legs worked too, and he would use them right now to get away from Traveling Towers. Free living? Huh! It cost too much misery in the end. From now on he would find his *own* food. Pagoo stamped a foot. Old Instinct didn't laugh. He didn't say "I *told* you this layout would be too fancy for you!"

The Landlady, knocked half out of her house by that last fall,

A SEA URCHIN TRAVELS IN SEARCH OF FOOD.
HAIR-FINE TUBE FEET EXTEND AND HOLD WITH SUCTION CUPS,
FRONT SPINES SHORTEN, REAR SPINES LENGTHEN AS IT CLIMBS.

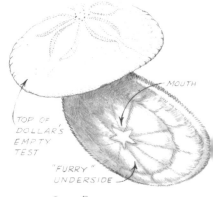

PAGOO EXPLORES
EMPTY TEST OF
URCHIN

TOP OF
DOLLAR'S
EMPTY
TEST

MOUTH

"FURRY"
UNDERSIDE

LIVING SAND DOLLARS ARE COVERED
WITH HAIR-LIKE SPINES. EDGING ALONG
UNDER THE SAND, THEY FIND THEIR FOOD.

A PURPLE STARFISH
EATS A MUSSEL

STRONG AND ELASTIC TUBE FEET
ENDING IN SUCTION CUPS, CAN
PULL A BI-VALVE'S SHELLS APART

saw her top roomer crawl out of the attic, clump downstairs, and stagger away. This was her first close look at Pagoo. A sweet little thing he was, good enough to eat—but, too exhausted to lift a feeler, she watched a battered Pagoo leave Traveling Towers.

He hid in the sand, and soaked up delicate sea-soup. He slid under seaweed and found bits of food. A five-inch fish who tried to eat Pagoo chased him under an empty Abalone Shell, and raced along its row of portholes trying to follow him in. The shell was small for an Abalone, but Pagoo was like a sparrow in an airplane hangar. There was plenty of room. Under this pearly dome Pagoo molted again. Though he came out a little bigger, he needed a shell—a Snail Shell—a *small* Snail Shell!

From a porthole Pagoo looked out on another part of the tide pool. Empty "tests" of dead Sea Urchins were hollow balls. Living Urchins lay in rock-pit beds, or were pulled along by tube-feet stretching between rows of prickly spines. Sand Dollars hid their furry discs under the sand, and Urchins swung their spines forward like spears, when an enemy Starfish came past. Star, Urchin, and Dollar were not-so-friendly first cousins, but none of them knew it, and Pagoo didn't care. What he wanted was a new home. He took to exploring old skeleton tests of these three cousins, trying to find a small, snug, and safe apartment.

Of the sea creatures Pagoo had met, only the fishes hid their skeletons inside themselves. The others, including himself, grew skeletons outside for protection. Pagoo climbed into an empty Urchin test, through the opening where its mouth had been. With all its spines and tube-feet off, it rolled like a ball in the currents till Pagoo grew dizzy inside and staggered out. The Sand Dollar test looked like a flat clay cooky, its opening too small for Pagoo. But he did bang his way into an empty Star. He walked inside where countless Mussels had disappeared, and he was not afraid. This dead Star had been washed near shore, and its five-winged skeleton had drifted aimlessly among

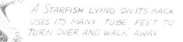

A STARFISH LYING ON ITS BACK
USES ITS MANY TUBE FEET TO
TURN OVER AND WALK AWAY

old Mussel shells. Many small hungry creatures had cleaned out the inside, leaving it quite vacant. Each empty arm was like the last, and Pagoo was confused.

Exploring such hollow spaces got Pagoo no nearer to finding a small home. From his porthole he could watch the changing things of the tide pool being swept into drifts that crept and crawled and turned endlessly over in tidal currents. He saw slivers of water-soaked driftwood, smoothly sanded; stems, blades, and old air-floats shredded from kelp; cement tubes made by Snails and certain Sea Worms; torn blobs of squishy Sponges; rows of Barnacle tepees knocked from rocks —all rolling aimlessly. But what caught Pagoo's bright eyes was the gleam of shells. There were Mussel, Abalone, Scallop, Limpet, Clam, and Snail Shells. SNAIL SHELLS? Yes! And when he saw them, Pagoo scooted through an open porthole, hoping, hoping. . . .

But this was Tide-pool Town, with a housing shortage. When poor Pagoo got to the shells, they were taken. More washed in every day, but the same thing happened. Peeking into shell doorways, he was switched by feelers, smacked by gloves, or he got a foot in his face. All he was after was a little shell; any little shell would do, for now. Battered away from the best places, he slunk off—but he wouldn't give up. He even poked into holes in wood, into Worm-tubes, into Barnacle silos, though he had no deep desire to live in another Barnacle house. Even these were taken. NO VACANCIES!

It was very discouraging, but he always could zip back to his pearl-domed hangar and settle under the quiet sands inside. That is, until one day he met a Worm—with too many legs. It came weaving in and out of his row of portholes. He watched—but this Worm wasn't searching for a house. *This* Worm was *hungry!* Pagoo waited for the last dozen legs to wade through a hole, then he left his Abalone Shell. No matter how shining and gleaming and gorgeous it was with rainbow colors, that arching pearly dome could become a trap. . . .

4 6

FROM HIS PORTHOLE PAGOO COULD WATCH THE TIDE POOL.

11. A CONCRETE TILE CAN CRAWL BOTH WAYS

ONCE AGAIN Pagurus was looking for a home. He hiked into Tide-pool Town, kicking at every Snail Shell, but all were occupied. He found an inch-long tube, a hollow concrete tile built by a Tube Snail. It had come from a tangled mass of tubes cemented to a rock by a colony of Snails who stay home and eat sea-soup. Pagoo tapped the tube, felt around one empty end, and snapped into it quickly.

Inside, this place was smoother than his penthouse Barnacle, and comfortable. Pagoo could drag this tube-home where he wished while hunting food. He didn't have to depend on a landlady, he wasn't trapped under a pearly dome. Pagoo rested. . . .

For no reason, the tube began moving. Pagoo stretched out his claws and front feet, dug into the sand to anchor things, and the tube stopped. This was very odd. No large animal was around, no danger seemed near, yet the tube had moved. Why should Pagoo be nervous —he who already had been Sculpin-swallowed, gull-hoisted, hard-beach-walloped? He jumped out and ran to the other end of the tunnel.

He found the other end stuffed with feelers. Two small gloves showed Pagoo that another Hermit lived there—a Hermit just his size, who did not seem glad to see him. In fact, this roomer at the other end of the hall pinched Pagoo. *Hard.*

Then Pagoo remembered that he was Pagurus, a two-fister built for fighting. The trouble was, this other fellow was a two-fisted fighter, too. They locked in mighty battle, a pair of polka dots punching each other. Both were so interested in fighting that Pagoo's opponent forgot to cling to his smooth, straight tube, and Pagoo snatched him into the open. Around and around they fought, rather careful of their tender rears, until a fish-shadow swooped down at them. Then each dashed into an end of the tunnel. They had switched ends, but that didn't matter now. Both retreated until they were touching back to back in

EMPTY SHELLS
OF TUBE SNAILS

the hallway, their trusty weapons covering both open doors. They seemed ready to fight together against the world.

But fighting together against the world is not for Hermit Crabs. Hermits seldom do things together, and these two certainly did not show teamwork. When Pagoo wished to travel in one direction the hall mate stubbornly crawled the other way, so both dug into the tidepool floor and pulled until something came loose. Sometimes Pagoo was hauled from his end, sometimes his hall partner was dragged out. After fisticuffs they would return to the hall, lean out from their separate doorways and start walking again—in different directions, of course. It was easier when both wanted to graze on the same algae-covered rock. Then for once they worked together like two oxen, dragging the Snail-tube sidewise like a yoke between them. But mostly they squabbled and fought, and little by little Pagoo proved himself the stronger. At last he was dragging the tube *his* way, while the other gave up and went along for the ride. It was hard on Pagoo, but it made his tiny body stronger still.

At each bracing new tide, Hermit Crabs came alive to tangle in happy boxing games. Hermits of one size were matched together, so that many classes and weights were going at once, as in a big gymnasium. The prizes were Snail Shell trunks. With young Hermits always growing and molting and needing new trunks half a size larger, old trunks were forever being tossed off and new ones tried on. As in a game of Musical Chairs, someone would be left with no pants to sit in. In one of these friendly battles, Pagoo grabbed a SHELL!

He had dragged his unwilling hall mate across the arena to mix in a scuffle with Hermits his size, and the gloves were going in a water-flurry beautiful to see! When many fighters had changed places, Pagoo was left near a Horn Shell, tapered like a trumpet. Its owner had left it to try on a new one for size, decided against that, and dashed home —right into Pagoo. Pagoo leaped, blocking the other's rush. Holding the other off, he popped his own curved rear into that Horn Shell.

At last Pagoo was *in!* Not in a rounded shell as yet, for this graceful beauty was shaped like a toy tin horn. But it had been made by a sure-enough Snail that walked on a foot—and it fitted Pagoo. No more of this dragging somebody around wherever he went. This shell made him safe from behind. When his larger glove plugged the doorway and his smaller glove covered the peekhole that was left, Pagoo was as snug as a pickle corked up in a bottle.

So Pagoo was suddenly secure—on his own—independent. Yes, he owned a castle that doubled as a house-trailer. How light it was, how easily handled. He zoomed up a steep rock, banged down a canyon of sensitive Mussels, and braked just in time to miss hitting—Traveling Towers! Ah-ha, so some stranger now had his old penthouse! Silly boy, he needn't expect free meat for every dinner—but let the dimwit find that out for himself. And the fat old Landlady? Loping along with the load, as usual. Remember little PAGOO? Look—LOOK at him NOW! But she only plodded on.

Pagoo made his trailer perky again with a burst of speed. He stopped at the worn old Snail-tube. He glimpsed a new roomer where he had so recently lived. But for his own quick wit, Pagoo himself might still be there!

Ah, Pagoo was the quick, the clever, the strong one with the sleek new outfit! He stared at his old hall mate and motioned him to come on out and fight. Clenching his claws, he waggled his eyes, and then, in mounting excitement, Pagoo did a very rash thing. He hopped right out of his brand-new shell and fairly pranced around in victory. Immediately he knew that he shouldn't have done it. Something rushed past him. What? How? Oh, *NO!* His old partner had grabbed Pagoo's new shell, was even now swishing his feelers in a gesture of triumph! And a rowdy Hermit gang was coming at Pagoo. He had to retreat, right back into that *same old tube.* . . .

5 0

PAGOO DRAGGED HIS UNWILLING HALL MATE ACROSS THE ARENA.

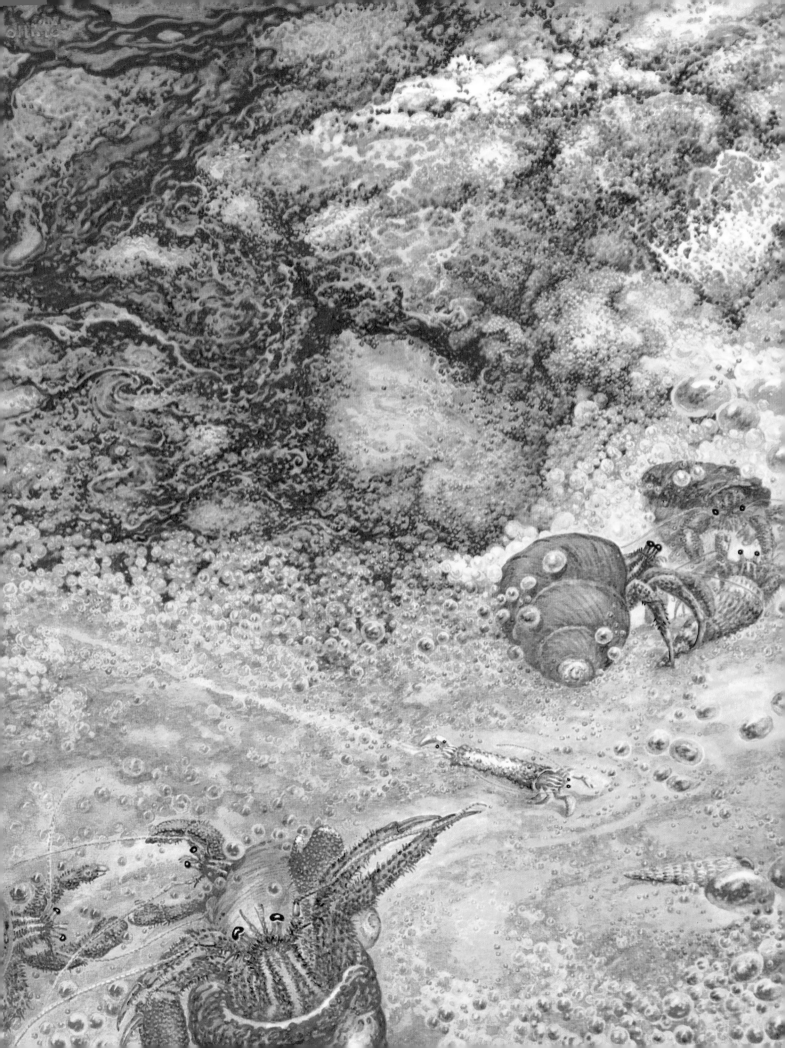

12. HERMIT HOUSE FROM AN ANCIENT JUNGLE

SAD PAGOO was right back where he started. He sulked in the Snail-tube, glaring at the world. True, this tube was the first home he had moved around all by himself. Even with a hall mate dragging his feet, it had been home. But after one glorious gallop in that Horn Shell—ah, that had been living! Now the Horn Shell was gone, lost— no, it was stolen by that ungrateful guy he had lugged all over the place. Why, Pagoo could lick him, high tide or low, with *one* claw only! But not any more. The fellow was safe—in Pagoo's very own shell. . . .

Pagoo's spirits were low for another reason besides the loss of his new shell. He was about to molt again. He crawled from his old tunnel, began a big wrestling match with himself, and finally kicked off his clinging test. When his armor was off he made a discovery—he couldn't go home. Already he had expanded far beyond his former size. Pagoo was too large now to fit in the same old concrete tile. Soft and wrinkled all over, his new armor wouldn't harden for a while. He must lie low, out of sight. He scuttled up a rock and hid in the crack of a ledge.

Of late, Pagoo's life had been held down to the tide-pool floors by the bulk of the Snail-tube, and the weight of his hall mate. For a long time he had not explored the spaces above. While in the Horn Shell, he had galloped about too rapidly to see much of the scenery. Waiting here in the crack, Pagoo met some new creatures.

He had thought all the bumps on the rocks were Limpets, but now he noticed one that was different. This Chiton (*ky*-ton) slid on its foot like a Limpet but its hard shell was shingled in eight sections. Pagoo saw a Chiton that a Starfish had pulled from a rock and then, for some Starry reason, had left behind. It lay cupped, a "sea cradle," all pink inside. Pagoo scuttled forward to see better, but the Chiton rolled into a ball and rocked in the waves.

Several lazy Sea Cucumbers lolled around, looking like sunburned

THE EIGHT-PLATED CHITON (PRONOUNCED KY'-TON) MAY BE LESS THAN AN INCH OR MORE THAN A FOOT LONG

"BUTTERFLY SHELL" FOUND ON THE BEACH IS ONE OF A CHITONS PLATES

GILLS — MANTLE — GIRDLE — MOUTH — FOOT

"SEA CRADLE"

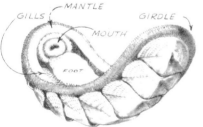

THIS CHITON, COUSIN OF SNAILS AND LIMPETS, CURLS UP FOR PROTECTION WHEN FORCED FROM ITS ROCK

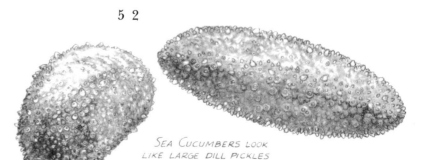

SEA CUCUMBERS LOOK LIKE LARGE DILL PICKLES

dill pickles left over from a picnic. These Cucumbers even had lumps and bumps. Compared to little Pagoo, they were larger than elephants. As he watched, Pagoo saw one end of each Cucumber unfold into a crown of filmy, branching tentacles for gathering food. Along bottom rows of lumps and bumps, tube-feet popped out as the animals moved slowly away in the usual search for food. These spiny-skinned Cucumbers were tube-footed cousins of Stars, Urchins, and Dollars.

BLOSSOM-LIKE TENTACLES
GATHER UP BITS OF FOOD

After a moment or two of snoozing, Pagoo was startled by whip-like arms romping over him in a great hurry. Five of these wiggly arms grew out of a little disc that looked like a fur-covered cookie. This small Serpent Star was still *another* cousin of the spiny-skinned Star, Urchin, Cucumber, and Dollar clan.

Being a shy creature in bright sunlight, this little Brittle (or Serpent) Star liked to come out only after dark. Today some Worm must have nudged this one out from under its protecting rock. If an enemy had caught it by one of its brittle, serpent-like arms, that arm would break off. The rest of it might escape, but for a long time this Brittle Star would hide away while it waited for another arm to grow.

Pagoo had seen these wiggly animals as dim shadows on nights when the tide was out. They would pull themselves up over the wet rocks, exploring with sensitive arms for bits of food. Pagoo glimpsed this lively fellow's mouth, on the under side of the furry disc. He saw the rows of spines and tube-feet along its squirming arms. Then it darted back to hide again, away from the bright sunlight.

BRITTLE STARS WIGGLE AND PULL
THEMSELVES OVER THE ROCKS
IN SEARCH OF FOOD AT LOW TIDE

Pagoo came out from his crack to lunch on a tidbit which came drifting down. Like all the Crab clan, Pagoo relished almost any kind of meat. But he could never know that, along with Brittle Stars, Cucumbers, Snails, and others, he was part of the "clean-up squad" of Tide-pool Town.

Pagoo returned to the safety of his crack at the edge of the rocky ledge. Not far below him a flowery garden was unfolding as he watched. He looked down into flowers that were not flowers. They, too, were

5 3

BRITTLE STAR

animals—with petal-like tentacles spread to capture food. They glowed in the water, lavender-pink and green. They had lived here for a very long time. These Sea Anemones had imitated flowers in this place for a hundred, two, or even more than three hundred years! With few enemies, they seemed able to live for ever.

These animal-flowers are greedy for all kinds of fleshy foods. Hermits are quick enough to race across spread-out petals and escape. Pagoo could not remember, but two large Hermit boxers had once dragged him safely across one of these traps. Now he saw a fat Snail feeding on a strand of kelp below him, and a Hermit Crab stumbling over the rock behind the Snail. The Hermit slipped, clutching the Snail for balance. Then Hermit and Snail, wearing the same kind of shell, tumbled down together into an open Anemone.

The Hermit leaped up and danced away, but he had to hurry. Already stinging-tentacle petals were curving upward, and he had to break through them like a pig crashing a green picket fence. The Snail was doomed. It was frightened by its fall and, snail-like, hugged itself into its shell for protection. Flowery petals folded over it. As though the Anemone had pulled a drawstring, all tentacles disappeared inward. This animal had gulped the Snail and was a bright flower no longer. Now it was nothing but a muddy-looking bulge with a dimple at the center to show where the Snail had gone.

The Anemone has a powerful tenderizer which can digest most Snails, but does not harm the shells. As Pagoo watched, he saw another Anemone tossing out a shell after the Snail inside it had been digested. That puckered Anemone, an untidy blob, now unfolded into a delicate blossom! As the lavender-pink petals uncurled, Pagoo saw the empty shell roll out clean and shiny and drop to the tide-pool floor. Once again, as it had through uncounted years, an Anemone animal, with no urge to help anyone but its own hungry self, had made a new home ready for some Hermit Crab. This time that Hermit *might* be Pagoo!

5 4

THIS ANIMAL HAD GULPED THE SNAIL
AND WAS A FLOWER NO LONGER.

13. THE GROTTO OF EATING TREES

PAGOO felt that he must go after that Snail Shell. He had seen it pop from the center of the Sea Anemone, and had watched it roll from that gay "flower" to the tide-pool floor beneath. He raced down the rock to search for it. He came to the place where the other Hermit had slipped and fallen. Weeds slid out from under him and broke loose —he couldn't hang on—he, too, was slipping! Directly below him stood the same Anemone which had swallowed a Snail before his very eyes. But it was still tightly closed and did not spread its tentacles to snare him. He bounced on its rubbery bulges and dropped to the floor.

All about him crowded an ancient, fantastic jungle. Anemones reared above Pagoo like stout palm trees of blazing colors. In the watery sunlight their fronds seemed to be jeweled and gilded. Pagoo walked on the sandy floor in swirls of liquid gold and shadow. With those rainbow colors arching above, the witchery of the place might have enchanted a more sensitive soul, but Pagoo was made of sterner stuff. He was not struck with the staggering beauty around him—he just staggered, that way, to keep under cover. He *must* find that new empty Snail Shell.

Sneaking along with his tail part tucked under, Pagoo blundered into a fairy cave. The rock walls of this dusky grotto were hidden beneath a crowded forest of growth. The roof was hung with ferns and bushes growing upside down. Pale, lacy nets of growth spread out near blooming mosses. This mysterious grotto seemed fairly alive with shadows. And the place *was* alive in more ways than one.

Things were not what they might seem to be. The blooming moss, the lacy nets, the hanging ferns and bushes were really colonies of very small animals. Most of these Bryozoan (bry-o-zo-an) colonies look like plants—each animal budding out from its neighbor. But each traps its own sea-soup food, using rings of slender tentacles.

AN ANCIENT ANEMONE JUNGLE

IN THE CAVE GREW
BRYOZOANS.
(BRY-O-ZŌ'-ANS)

NET-LIKE PATCHES
CLUNG TO THE ROCK

5 6

FERN-LIKE CLUSTERS HUNG
FROM THE ROOF

TO PAGOO, CLOSE UP,
THESE PLANT-LIKE COLONIES OF ANIMALS
BLOSSOMED WITH WAVING TENTACLES

BUSH-LIKE GROWTHS
CROWDED THE FLOOR

Just as trees tower above underbrush, other animals here stretched above the Bryozoans. These Hydroid (hy-droyd) colonies were also built by hundreds of tiny creatures growing in orderly rows. Some Hydroids grow like slender palms with waving plumes. Each animal traps food for the colony with stinging tentacles. Pagoo once had traveled with children of Hydroid families—tiny Medusa (me-*du*-sa) Jellyfish. Medusas pop gaily away from their stay-put family tree, join the sparkling plankton ballet for a generation, and even have baby jellies who can swim. But *these* babies, as though bored with the life of their wandering parents, return to shore. They settle down and start stay-at-home Hydroid colonies like the original family homestead.

Pagoo found what he was after in this Grotto of Eating Trees! He found not only one Snail Shell, but a whole treasure of shells! Since the Anemone jungle sloped down to the grotto, shells dropped by Anemones or brought by waves rolled into the cave. Here were Snail Shells of many kinds and sizes. And all these Snail Shells were EMPTY!

"Well!" said Old Pal. "So little old Pagoo has hit the jackpot!"

Was it all a dream? Pagoo didn't know where to start. He began trying on one shell after another, in a frenzy of joy. But at last Old Pal got an idea into Pagoo. "Look, boy!" he cried. "After all, you can wear only *one* shell. So find that *one*."

A fat little Periwinkle Shell fitted Pagoo. His small soft body curled into its curves as though made for this place. The door was too wide, but with both gloves he could close the opening fairly well. Pagoo did not start running in wild loops as he had done with his first Snail Shell, the Horn. With dignity he walked from the deep, hidden Grotto of Eating Trees, and sat on a stone. Here the little fish found him.

Since bringing meat that time to the Landlady of Traveling Towers, the small-mouthed fellow had used any Crustacean at all to shred meat for him. He towed meat to Shrimps, and left those pale creatures to work on it. Shore Crabs, Swimmer Crabs, any Crabs at all were very useful, just so long as they didn't catch and shred *him* along with the

HYDROIDS
(HY-'DROYDS)
"THE EATING TREES"

A ME-DU'-SA HYDROID

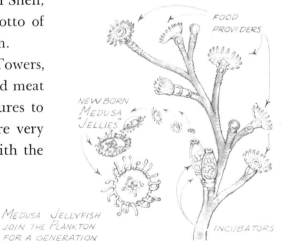

FOOD
PROVIDERS

NEW BORN
MEDUSA
"JELLIES"

INCUBATORS

STAY-AT-HOME COLONY

MEDUSA JELLYFISH
JOIN THE PLANKTON
FOR A GENERATION

ANOTHER HYDROID SEEMED COVERED
WITH PINK AND WHITE BLOSSOMS

A TIDE-POOL BLENNY

meat. Sometimes a huddle of Shrimps didn't understand when he dashed back to claim his tiny morsels. Shrimps exploded in all directions—but they came back. The small fish kept everyone satisfied.

Pagoo was so startled when the small fellow swished up to him that he crouched far back in his shell and put up both gloves. When he looked out, there lay a nice piece of steak—and a job to do. He cut and shredded that Scallop meat for all that he was worth. If Hermit Crabs can feel flattered, Pagoo should have felt a warmish glow, even in cold ocean water. To be given a job like this to work on meant that young Pagoo now was large enough to be noticed! He wasn't sitting upstairs in old Traveling Towers, watching the Landlady below and hoping. Pagoo himself was carving! Of course he ate his share.

He did so well that he sprayed meat particles all over the scenery. Tidal currents caught them up and carried the news around the corners. Not only the small fish returned, but hungry Shrimps, hungry Worms, hungry Hermits. Hermits in all sizes! Pagoo had rested from Hermit fights of late, and had almost forgotten the rude ways of his own tribe. Clutching as much steak as his claws could hold, Pagoo retreated. He scuttled toward his Grotto of Eating Trees, his new Periwinkle Shell bumping along behind.

All the gang followed. They clawed and pulled at Pagoo's tasty lunch. They knocked his little shell around, reached into his too-wide doorway, and pinched him with no mercy at all. He tried to block that doorway—but his gloves were much too small. And he had no more chances to taste the feast he had so carefully prepared. Pagoo had learned something, and Old Instinct made it a fact by saying, "Yep, you may be a *little* larger after that last molting, but not yet *large!*"

It was only too true. As yet, he could not hold his own against the big boys. And this doorway—why hadn't he chosen a better shell? That hole was much too wide! Oh, well, when this rumpus was over, he would go back there and get another house with an opening he liked. He knew where he could get it. Pagoo almost smiled.

5 8

PAGOO FOUND A WHOLE TREASURE OF SHELLS.

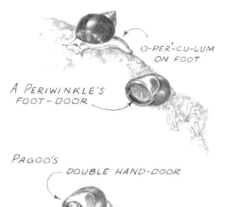

O-PER'-CU-LUM ON FOOT

A PERIWINKLE'S FOOT-DOOR

PAGOO'S DOUBLE HAND-DOOR

14. AMONG THE CRABS, A SHY MASKED LADY

AFTER the Hermits had stolen Pagoo's lunch, they barged on into his secret cave. Scufflings started, kept on and on. When all was quiet again, Pagoo looked in upon disaster. The Hermit gang had departed, but the foliage of his grotto was torn and scattered. Pagoo cared little about this, but his hidden treasure—*his* shells—ROBBED! The best ones had vanished! Only cracked and battle-worn shanties had been left—old wrecks tossed away by the raiders as junk. Disgusted, Pagoo looked them all over but found none as good as his own wide-door Periwinkle. Pagoo's red feelers lashed in rage! But Old Pal grunted, "Simmer down! Nature will fix things!" And, sure enough, with the very next molt the trouble was neatly fixed. Pagoo's large claw had grown larger, so that his right hand became a very good door.

It was not a real door, of course, like that of many Sea Snails. A Snail's door, or operculum (o-*per*-cu-lum), is a horny shield grown to fit its doorway. As the Snail hauls itself into its shell the operculum comes last, on the tip of the foot. It seals the opening against almost anything except, perhaps, the Anemone. Compared to this foot-door, Pagoo's hand-door did not have such a snug fit. A peekhole remained, to be covered by his small left claw. Yet even with the peekhole open, his right glove now saved Pagoo from meddlesome bullies.

Through that peekhole under his hand-door Pagoo could watch his Crab relations. Many tribes of them lived in Tide-pool Town. The deepest places held Swimming Crabs, whose two rear feet had widened into swim-fins. Near shore, most Crabs are not swimmers, but walkers like Pagoo. Some Shore Crabs are at home in water or on land.

Once when the tide had ebbed and the pool was calm, Pagoo walked his shell close to the edge of land. He saw Shore Crabs in the water clearly, but when they broke through the surface-window they vanished for a moment. Then the shattered window wobbled itself

6 0

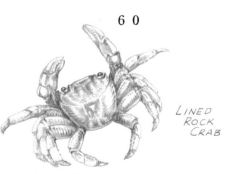

PURPLE SHORE CRAB

LINED ROCK CRAB

PORCELAIN
CRAB

COMMERCIAL
CRAB

SWIMMING
CRAB

together, and he saw them above water, on the rocks. It was as though you looked into an aquarium—only backward. Crabs on land seemed all wiggly to Pagoo under water. Sometimes they were only shadows, like sand tossed along by the wind on the beach.

Some Shore Crabs are large, with heavy claws of great gripping power. If one of these Crabs could be the size of a Strong Man in a circus, he could crunch steel railroad tracks like sticks of candy, and rip up a battleship's anchor chains like picking beans! No wonder little Pagoo kept inside his shell when *they* came by!

He saw small Rock Crabs who also had pinchers. Their bodies flat and thin enough to crawl into cracks or under rocks, every Crab seemed to fit his living space so that he could hide easily. But certain Crabs put on *masks* to hide from their enemies! When old, they are huge, wear thick armor, and do not have to hide. But while younger, they wear masks—and seem to disappear, as Pagoo found out.

One day Pagoo walked his shell into the open, toward a garden of swaying weeds. He was almost past when a clump of the weeds raised up at a crazy angle, and under it somewhere he saw the beady eyes of a Crab. A Crab hiding in weeds was only natural, but these seaweeds appeared to be growing right out of this Crab's back! She was a shy young lady Crab with legs that looked much too long (and *lumpy,* too)! And she certainly was having a bit of trouble with them.

Ah-ha! Pagoo knew what was going on—or, rather, what was coming off. This lady was molting! He watched as things began to happen along her back. Its outer layer came loose and tilted up, weeds growing on the crust of it. The lady gave a quick, many-legged kick, and sent her hanging garden up and away for tides to play with. No doubt about it—this timid Crab cousin, with her soft new body and spidery legs, now had nothing at all to hide her.

She scuttled among curling rockweeds and slender eelgrass. Exploring with claws and feelers, she worked over the hold-fast bases of several plants. At last, finding one to please her, she pried it up and

61

DECORATOR CRAB
MOLTING

cut it loose, ready for transplanting. Her mouth furnished a special glue, which now she used to paste the plant's hold-fast to the knobby new covering on her back. She needed several rear legs, both claws, and one feeler to do this trick, but at long last she got it finished. The seaweed, glued tightly to her back, would continue to grow gaily.

This "Decorator Crab" became a masked lady as she kept on decorating herself. As Pagoo watched, she used several kinds of seaweeds, even strands of eelgrass. Every now and again she pulled up more feathery growth, pasting it over joints of her long legs. The Decorator didn't care that these Bryozoans on her elbows ate sea-soup, just so they grew lacy veils to hide her gangling legs and arms.

Pagoo passed Snail Cousins' Rock, climbed Mussel Ridge, took a long and shuddery look at pale rope-like things waving in Deep Hole, and skittered back again. Where was the Lady Decorator? He stared hard at a wavy garden of weeds, but it wasn't *her* garden. He backed into other weeds, hoping to find her, but ready to run in case he *did* touch her and make her feel insulted. The weeds seemed to be empty! All this time, close by under rocking, waving fronds, the Lady was watching him. In the open tide pool, she was quite well hidden.

Pagoo paused among rounded boulders. Green Rock Crabs with yellow lines across their backs were hunting bits of food in the algae. They ate busily, using one claw, then the other, but always with eyes alert to any change in scenery. They ran sidewise up a rock, slipped through the surface-window without breaking it, and continued to poke for food on the boulders above. The Rock Crabs stared down at Pagoo, and he stared up—till a brisk wave shattered the window. One by one some busy diners slipped down, slid their eyes through the foam, and peered below. Yes, Pagoo's fat little shell still rocked in the undertow on the tide-pool floor, like a cradle rocking in a nursery. For the Rock Crabs it was good to know that the old tide-pool home was still there—that the last wave hadn't washed it away. And for Pagoo it was comfortable to be rocking gently in the swinging sea.

THE ROCK CRABS STARED DOWN AT PAGOO.

15. PAGOO TAKES A SHELL—KEEPS IT, TOO

PAGURUS was growing. With every swish of incoming tide, with every gurgle of the ebb, he had grown a little bit. Tide in, tide out, there came a time when he molted again, flexed his muscles, and found his shell too tight. This good old Periwinkle Shell would not serve Pagoo much longer. Since this last molt, the little shell covered only about half of him. It was still a pair of trunks, but he could no longer withdraw behind his handy door to take a snooze.

Once more Pagoo bumped into Tide-pool Town, looking for a larger shell. All he had to do was to spot one the right size, and if he could get it no other way, he would fight for it. He'd take on any big bruiser! With his knobby new skin-armor he felt strong enough to lick anything. His larger size gave Pagoo this confidence. He still held his weapons ready, but he kept right on going and entered a seaweed alley. The light was dim. He stumbled over dumps of shells, but not a single one that he could use. He kicked into an empty test which had once been a fat Crab, but a hungry gang had cleaned him out.

Pagoo swaggered on, slapping at weeds with new red feelers. At a corner, he ran smack into the arms of the Masked Lady. He side-stepped, bowing as though begging her pardon, but backing away all the time. Watching this Decorator don her mask out in the open was *one* thing, here in the dark was another, and after all, she had a *very* long reach, and—well, anyhow, he kept right on going!

Yes, Pagoo was growing up, because he still was quite calm and collected after glimpsing—around a bend—Big Head the Sculpin!

Yes sir, if you could see Big Head in time to dodge him, and then come out of the thickets without weak knees wobbling and feelers trembling, you were getting along toward being a real man-Crab! Pagoo acted as though he realized all this. He walked with a spring in his step, he felt good (though a bit cramped in his shell). He stopped to

OLD INSTINCT'S RULES
FOR CHOOSING A SHELL

gaze toward a glare of sunlight from an open square ahead. Small fry of Tide-pool zipped past his legs, heading for cover. Torn weeds sailed overhead, as though hurled from some big commotion. He felt, rather than heard, the collision and the clackety-clack of Snail Shells striking together. Over yonder was a hassle of Hermits, or his name wasn't Pagoo, and he certainly meant to get into the fun.

MAKE SURE THE FORMER
OWNER IS OUT —
HOW ABOUT SIZE ?
NOT TOO HEAVY ?

But—here was that old character Instinct again, and Pagoo had to listen. "Nope, don't mix in it. You *feel* big, but what have you done to show that you *are* big? Let's see—you ran into a Masked Lady, and walked away. You saw Big Head, far off—you just managed to *see* him —and you scooted for cover. Now you're about to enter a tussle, and offer to fight *any*body! Don't do it, lad. You're half out of your shell already, and no door to rest behind in a pinch. Those boys are really *big.* Better wait—at least till you find yourself a good shell to sit in. After that, well. . . ."

TURN IT OVER CAREFULLY—
LOOK AT IT FROM ALL SIDES

So Pagoo did not walk right over and leap into the fray. He skulked around the ring at the outside, dodging the spurts of sand shooting up from churning feet. It was quite a rough-and-tumble affair and, as usual Old Instinct was right. Oh, *why,* after every molting, did Pagoo feel big enough to lick the world? The fellows going at it here were husky—Pagoo would have been no match for them. He backed into a nook. Between two boulders, he was right on hand when a pile of battlers, plus some empty shells, rolled in a jumbled ball against the rocks nearby. In the confusion, a vacant shell—a wonderful, roomy Brown Turban Shell—lay before Pagoo.

REACH FAR INSIDE
WITH YOUR LONG RIGHT CLAW
BE SURE IT IS SAFE AND CLEAN
GIVE IT A TAP. LIKE THE SOUND ?

By all the rules, he ought to wait. He should grasp the wide opening and look in, like an old-time grocer examining a barrel for bad apples. He should twist and twirl it around, as though whirling the barrel to get a better light into the deep inside. He should use this feeler, that one, tapping and testing, reaching his arm in up to his shoulder. That's the way it is done in the best Hermit circles—when there is time. Pagoo didn't have time, but he did have the big shell,

6 5

NOW SEE IF IT FITS —
BUT MAKE IT SNAPPY !!
HOP OUT OF THE OLD ONE —
THEN TAIL-FIRST INTO THE NEW SHELL

and before the last owner could snatch it back, Pagoo was inside. *Way* inside! Certain it was, this shell was much too big for the likes of Pagoo, but he kept backing. The trouble was that the owner came backing in on top of him. Pagoo was being *sat* on.

There was only one thing to do, and of course Pagoo did it. Since he had captured this shell fairly, nobody was going to squat down on *him* and not know it! In quiet rage Pagoo reached his big pincher forward, took careful aim—and clamped down *hard*.

The other Hermit uttered no sound, of course, but he whooshed out of there like a rocket just touched off. His rear must have ached, his pride must have been hurt. At any rate he barged through the arena, bowling shells over right and left. He went away for good into the shadows, leaving Pagoo with a too large home to rattle around in.

Pagoo did not seem to mind that his home was too large. Some of the rowdy gangs bothered him at first. At any hour, day or night, characters came to his wide doorway thinking the Turban Shell was empty. He had a few fights (and won them, too), teaching the local toughs not to meddle. He hung out a THIS HOUSE TAKEN sign—his feelers. When he slid far forward, the ends of his feelers warned others away.

Getting around with this barn trailing behind was quite a chore. Pagoo was always on the lookout for a better-fitting shell, but none turned up. So he just sat around, rested, ate, and grew. Inside his home, Pagoo felt safe. His big right claw plus his small left, almost fitted the Brown Turban's curving hallway—far inside.

Tides washed in, leaving Tide-pool Town with several feet of sparkling cold water, bubbling with snow-white foam. The next time he molted, Pagoo did the whole job safely inside his shell, and kicked his old clothes out of the door. After that, when the wrinkles of his new skin filled in and his new crust hardened, he had a pleasant surprise. He did not have to go looking for a new home. He had grown to fit this one!

6 6

THE OTHER HERMIT SWOOSHED OUT OF THERE LIKE A ROCKET.

SHORT COMB-LIKE FEELERS
(AN-TEN´-NULES)

CLEANING BRUSHES

LONG WHIP-LIKE FEELER
(AN-TEN´-NA)

16. DEATH TRAP!

ONE AFTERNOON Pagoo felt restless, and unusually hungry. Was the sea-soup a bit weaker these days? Were plain vegetables growing tiresome? He simply wanted a steak—that was it! For a long time, now, the little fish had not delivered meat to be shredded. Pagoo could not even remember their last feast together. Perhaps the waves had dropped meaty leftovers in the upper tide pools? He would go up and see. But on top of a ledge above Tide-pool Town Pagoo saw no meat—and he noticed that the tide was ebbing. The ledge was already half out of water. He paused as if thinking.

Pagoo seemed to be whipping up new thoughts with his orange-red feelers—all four of them. Through his feelers he learned many things which his nearsighted eyes could not tell him. Of course his whip-like pair were for tapping, poking, exploring. But a second pair, so short that they might easily be overlooked, stuck out where Pagoo's nose should be. In a way, they took the place of a nose, though they looked like a pair of tiny red claws edged with fine hair-combs. These sensitive hairs gave him news of any change in the taste of water or the smell of air.

Tide in, tide out, Pagoo was forever testing ocean water. By now he was an expert at testing air. Under the midday sun of summer, his feelers had found dry air alarmingly hot, and warned him to duck under in a hurry. At night, or on a cool sunless day such as this, open air was not bad for a few minutes if he kept his gills wet. Raw air gave Pagoo a strangled feeling such as you might have after holding your breath too long while diving. But now, half out of water, his short feelers shouted that THIS air was different! It was not dry or hot, and it held a strange but pleasant dampness. It hinted at something BIG about to happen.

Pagoo snapped back into his shell as dark, swift forms flew low above Tide-pool Town. Perhaps he remembered a dizzy flight and narrow escape from the gull-monster who had scooped up Traveling Towers. But these birds were wild geese, not Hermit-hungry gulls. The long V of the flock wavered against the gray sky, and was gone. Pagoo's four feelers went back to batting again—just testing.

Pagoo sloshed across the watery ledge toward a small pool worn into the flat rock. He wanted deeper water, so he walked to the pool's rim and looked down. This gemlike pond was no larger than a baby's bathtub. Around its upper edge grew a lavender ruffle of algae like a fancy collar. Jaunty Pagoo stepped out on this fringe, hugged his body into his house, and let himself slide off. His shell made a faint tinkly sound as it rolled down the rocky slope of the pool.

He came to rest on the bottom among rounded pebbles. Such stones as these, washed round and about by waves for countless years, had gouged out this oval pool. Perhaps a rock-boring Clam had started it all by drilling a snug tunnel for itself in the solid ledge. After it died, waves had churned sand into the tunnel and widened it into a pit. Now each tide brought pebbles and boulders—swirling them, pounding them, grinding the small pit larger. In a few more centuries the surf might hollow a huge cave here.

Pagoo was interested only in this moment, for he had found his meat—a very limp Limpet, dead in its shell like a forgotten platter of steak. Pagoo didn't care that the steak was not at all fresh; he liked it that way. Holding the dish with his big right mitten he plucked out bite-sized pieces with his left, beginning around the edges.

While Pagoo ate, his eyes saw odd happenings above him. For no good reason the calm flat ceiling of the pool began to jiggle. Then great dents shattered the glassy skylight. The dents dug deeper, but each one seemed to explode and melt away in bubbles. Yet more dents came, faster, faster, like lances stabbing down. And, oddly, each stab of a new dent changed the taste of the pool's water, as Pagoo's short feelers soon found out. What *was* this, anyway?

From under the lavender ruffle at the pool's rim, several Snails appeared. Pagoo had not noticed them grazing there—now they came rolling down on him like marbles. Tucked into their shells, doors shut, tumbling down the slopes, they thumped him on all sides. Nearby Limpets only hugged their home bases more closely, clung more tightly to the rock. But tiny copepods darted about in the sea-soup like insect swarms gone completely crazy.

By these frantic signs and the fuss Old Instinct seemed to be making, Pagoo was awakened to danger. He long since had stopped eating. Now, from the fringes of his small feelers right down to the knobs and hairs on the rest of his body, he understood that something serious was happening. This rain pelting into the pool was rapidly changing the comfortable salted water into weak, unsalted stuff! Old Pal finally got through to Pagoo with the urgent message, "FRESH WATER WILL KILL YOU! GIT, SON—AND I MEAN *RIGHT NOW!*"

Pagurus dropped his plate of meat and ran. His first spurt took him halfway up the steep slope. He slowed, almost lost balance, curled a tighter tail-hold deep down inside his house, and climbed slowly on up—holding desperately with his very toenails. All but exhausted, he hugged his armor-plates over his gills and lunged with a super effort. He reached the ruffle of algae at the pool's rim. He clutched at the water plants and hauled himself, claw over claw, up through the layered branches. At last he fought his way out of that death pit and onto the flat rock ledge.

The salty ebb tide had flowed away, leaving the rock ledge bare. But now a new flood of *fresh* rain water came dashing across the ledge, washed down from the cliffs above. A thick torrent of rain spun Pagoo's shell, picked it up, and skidded it forward. Like a tiny canoe in a vast Niagara Falls, Pagoo's shell was tossed over the brim—and Pagoo went with it.

7 0

AS PAGOO WATCHED, THE DENTS GREW DEEPER.

17. A FRIGHT, A FROLIC, AND A FAREWELL

RAIN SPURTED over rocks and foamed across the tide pools—a fresh-water layer riding on top of the salty water of Tide-pool Town. Pagoo's shell, tossed from the ledge by the waterfall, bounced and skipped for an instant on the hissing layer of rain. When fresh and salt waters mingled, Pagoo lost speed and sank to the bottom.

At first there was a blankness of muddied water. Then Pagoo saw nightmares of frightened creatures rushing seaward—dim shapes of Crabs, Fishes, Shrimps, Worms, Lobsters. Swimmers and crawlers by the thousands were on the move to deeper places. They knew by instinct that unsalted water could kill them. Now this poisonous fresh-ness was *raining* down! Even Pagurus would have to hurry.

At a low part of Tide-pool Town, tired Pagoo dragged his shell down into a canyon. As the canyon deepened, fresh water grew weaker. Except for being elbowed by crowds on all sides of him, Pagoo felt safer here. But help for the overcrowding was at hand. Every twelve hours, rain *or* shine, the tide rolls in—and here it came. Strong new brine crept landward, making deep places deeper and more roomy. It salted the rain water in time to save those beings not already dead.

Night came and the rain was less violent, but a steady sea wind blew even harder. Pagoo and his neighbors felt their world shudder as billows surged over the canyon. Driftwood logs from northern beaches, timbers from long-wrecked ships hurtled shoreward like battering-rams, while ropes of kelp lashed about in the undertow.

Undertow grew strong as huge rollers crashed on the cliffs, rush-ing to sea again. Each flattened wave slid back under the next one, its tons of wild water ripping up sea bottom as it ran. This powerful undertow tugged at anything loose. It churned sand and pebbles, it juggled stones larger than baseballs, it hoisted bowling-ball sizes for new waves to bat about. Even barnacled boulders big as bus wheels were lifted and heaved at the cliffs. Undertow sucked gravel from beneath tall rocks, and waves pushed them over. Tide-pool scenery which had stood for years was shifted and changed.

Time and again, this night, Pagoo came near to his death. Old Pal had yelled, "Sit tight!" and Pagoo had sat. A log smashed into the canyon wall, starting a rockslide that buried a million beings. Pagoo clawed out of that gritty mess only to be tumbled and rolled by kelp snaking past. A load of gravel streaked by like buckshot, yet all of it missed Pagoo. His shell was buried in mud—washed up, buried in sand—dragged out, and then it slid under a boulder.

Pagoo edged farther under when a wave tilted the rock. When it teetered back CRUNCH! His shell was cracked like a nut, yet it held together. Pagoo was unharmed, but this wobbly boulder could no longer be trusted. He wiggled his shell out, found a sheltered place between a Crab and a Lobster, huddled there, and waited for this wild night to end.

The night ended, as all nights do, and the rain stopped. The storm blew itself out by sunup, but waves ran high and stones still rolled in the undertow. Food smells drifted everywhere. Pagoo left the Crab and the Lobster, hustled up the canyon, and hiked into Tide-pool Town. He marched among countless refugees returning. With speedy spurts and sidewise skitters they dodged the rolling stones. Those creatures still alive began feasting on those who were not, as is the ancient custom of the sea. Pagoo had just finished a plate of Clam when the undertow swirled him up, a wave caught him and rushed him ashore.

The wave carried him far up the beach and slammed him down on a rock. Noisy gulls flapped and feasted all around him, so this was no place for Pagoo. Besides, his landing had shattered his cracked shell. Now, like clothes being shed by a boy in a race to go swimming, Pagoo's covering dropped away from him, piece by piece. Only one small cup clung to his tail as he high-stepped down a retreating wave into Tide-pool Town—and even that fell off.

7 3

Bare Pagoo was badly in need of a home. After a storm is the very best time to look for seashells, and now a salmon-brown Wavy-Top caught his eye. Knobs, like pearls, bumped its crinkled surface. He liked it so well that he prodded it only a little and backed right in. He curled his rear around the shell's inner column. Everything seemed perfect.

It would have been wiser to make a longer inspection, but Pagoo was anxious to be on his way. This glittering mansion made him feel most important. He had grown beyond the boy Hermit stage—he was big and strong—and he certainly felt like celebrating this fine day. He elbowed into a picnic here, he sampled banquet dainties there, and all day long he swaggered through Tide-pool Town.

And so toward evening he wandered back to the old Hermit gang. He was fairly bursting to try out his new-found strength. Quick-witted sparring was going friendly enough until some low Hermit found a *hole*—right in the rear of Pagoo's handsome mansion. And the vulgar fellow stuck in his pointed toe—and poked!

Pagoo whooshed from that shell as another Hermit had done after young Pagoo pinched him. Yet instead of sulking, Pagoo turned and charged at the gang. Surprised at such sudden fury, each Hermit ducked inside and slammed his doors. This big boy meant business! This fellow was really on a tear! First one, then another of the gang felt his house lifted and banged down hard, and rolled like a bowling ball to crash against his neighbors. Why, this lad had become a raging billow, a mangling menace, The Terror of Tide-pool Town!

It could not last. Pagoo grew tired. Eyes began to peer out, huts and shanties flipped upright. Then it was as though someone yelled: LOOK, BOYS! AFTER ALL, IT'S ONLY PAGOO—AND UN-DRESSED, TOO! GET HIM!

Pagoo braced himself. He could face those charging from the front —but the thuds of the shell-gang coming behind him simply left him all unstrung. Clearly, it was time to go. With no heavy shell to slow his speed, Pagoo beat them all as they ran him out of town.

18. DOWN TO THE DEPTHS OF DEEP HOLE

THE LANDLADY halted her wobbling on Snail Cousins' Rock. Now who could that be, whizzing by her so fast? He pretty near upset Traveling Towers, he did! Headed for Mussel Ridge, looks like. If he doesn't slow up, Deep Hole is waiting next—last stop for rash young Hermits like *him*. Oh, well—here today, gone tomorrow. . . .

Landlady or no Landlady, Pagoo did not fall headlong into the Deep Hole—that is, not at first. The Hermit gang had given up chasing him, so he slowed to a stop on Mussel Ridge. Right here he had studied his first Mussels, he first had climbed a Barnacle. And over there at the edge of the rock, the purple Starfish had crept up toward him out of Deep Hole. Deep Hole! What was his fear of it? Pagoo crawled to the brink, braced himself on a lacy frond, and peered down.

One thing not needed at this jittery moment was Big Head the Sculpin. Yet here he came swooping, trailing bubbles, aiming straight for Pagoo. Those horrible jaws! Pagoo had passed through *that* gateway before—in and out. Now that he was about to be gulped again, this time he might have to stay inside! The awful mouth coming at him seemed to yawn wider than Deep Hole itself! Pagoo, flat on the lacy frond, clutched at one edge with two feet and a claw, leg muscles twitching in terror. His legs jerked him right under the edge and dangled him from the frond as Big Head swooshed over. Against the blue blankness of Deep Hole, the head-heavy fish with the tapering tail looked like a plane—a plane overshooting its target. It banked, it rolled, it returned full throttle. But where was that juicy little Hermit?

Pagoo's lacy frond was a dead section of an Eating Bush—a Bryozoan. His frantic dodging had snapped the stem off like a stick of candy. The brittle lace, Pagoo dangling from it, flopped over and over like a leaf, zigzagging down into the depths of Deep Hole.

Big Head slowed, twisted his body and followed the branch down.

His fidgety tail and pitchfork fins kept working in jerks, waiting for the hanging Pagoo to swing into range. But his timing was off as he charged the frond on a wrong turning, and Pagoo let go just as Big Head struck. The Sculpin scooped up a mouthful of stuff as crumbly as plaster, while Pagoo, losing his parachute, dropped like a stone. Big Head, near the surface, was still groping about in a flurry of torn lace when Pagoo struck bottom, far below. It was a soft mud bottom, handy for landing in and digging under backward. Pagoo dug.

Disgusted Big Head vanished to higher tide pools. When he did not return, Pagoo raised himself from the mud. So this was Deep Hole he had dreaded! With Big Head gone, what was left to dread? Pagoo noticed that Mussels were larger here. As if to go with the larger Mussels, he saw a whopping big Starfish tube-footing his way across the bare sea bottom. Starfish were old stuff to Pagoo. Yet he jerked into the mud again when a shadow moved in the weeds.

"Nope," said Old Instinct at his elbow. "Don't you fear that Moray Eel. He looks horrible, but he's nearsighted, and doesn't bother Hermits. Morays are after that thing with the *long* arms you haven't seen yet—but you'll know soon enough. . . . Now stay put, son," he said chattering on. The time passed by so slowly.

Old Instinct had become quite boring. "Stay put," he had advised. But Pagoo left. He squeezed himself up from the sticky mud, plowed a furrow across it to a great standing rock, and began cleaning himself. He scrubbed and he rubbed and he whisked with bristles, and he came out fresh and new again. He had just brushed the knob of a knee for its final polish, when one wandering eye showed him— a SHELL!

"Watch out!" called Instinct, but Pagoo smothered the call, for beyond that shell lay another, *another*, ANOTHER—a path of Snail Shells leading around the base of the rock. Pagoo dropped his cleaning brushes and all his caution, and trailed those shells like a hound after rabbits, around the rock to HEAPS OF SHELLS.

7 7

Shades of the Grotto of Eating Trees! He had found a new grotto, a cave dented under the base of the rock. Only this time the shells lay not in the hollow, but out in the open for him to examine! As though something had pushed them out of the cave just for him, they lay outside like a motionless wave of hard, bubbly froth. Pagoo waded into that crisp froth, the shells rolling every which way.

Pagoo stood up to his upper knees in treasures, busy as busy, trying them on for size. This one—no, that one—no, that over there —the black one, the Turban with the sparkly, pearly top—oh, he did like that one. This time he made sure there were no hidden holes before he stepped in. Snug. Perfect! It put that bright ending to Pagoo, that elegant, finishing touch.

"Finishing touch is right! Son, I've been trying to *tell* you something. Yes, I know you needed that shell, but your fool's luck won't hold much longer! Scoot!"

Pagoo gave little heed. He was sleepy. Daylight was being turned off upstairs, the big round sun had gone out as usual. Layers of darkness were settling down in Deep Hole, and tiny, twinkling lights of the sea were coming on. Far up at the surface, luminous flecks were dancing. Farther down, weed fronds waved sparklers. . . .

Tired, Pagoo merely glanced at the fireworks and turned toward the cave. He had had a very busy day. He would just walk into this quiet cave—but what was in here? He saw a faint glow at the back, becoming a shape like a great pale moon in a mist, a monstrous egg in a nest of long, pale, ropy, wiggly things!

Pagoo moved sidewise so slowly he seemed not to move at all. He edged into a dark crack. He pushed his shell far back, he stuffed himself farther back in his shell, he strained backward. He didn't want to look out—but of course his eyes would not shut. Those pale, wriggling things out there were tentacles! Old Instinct did not have to shout—Pagoo knew. Deep Hole held an ancient enemy of Hermits, this *Octopus!*

THOSE PALE, WRIGGLING THINGS OUT THERE WERE TENTACLES!

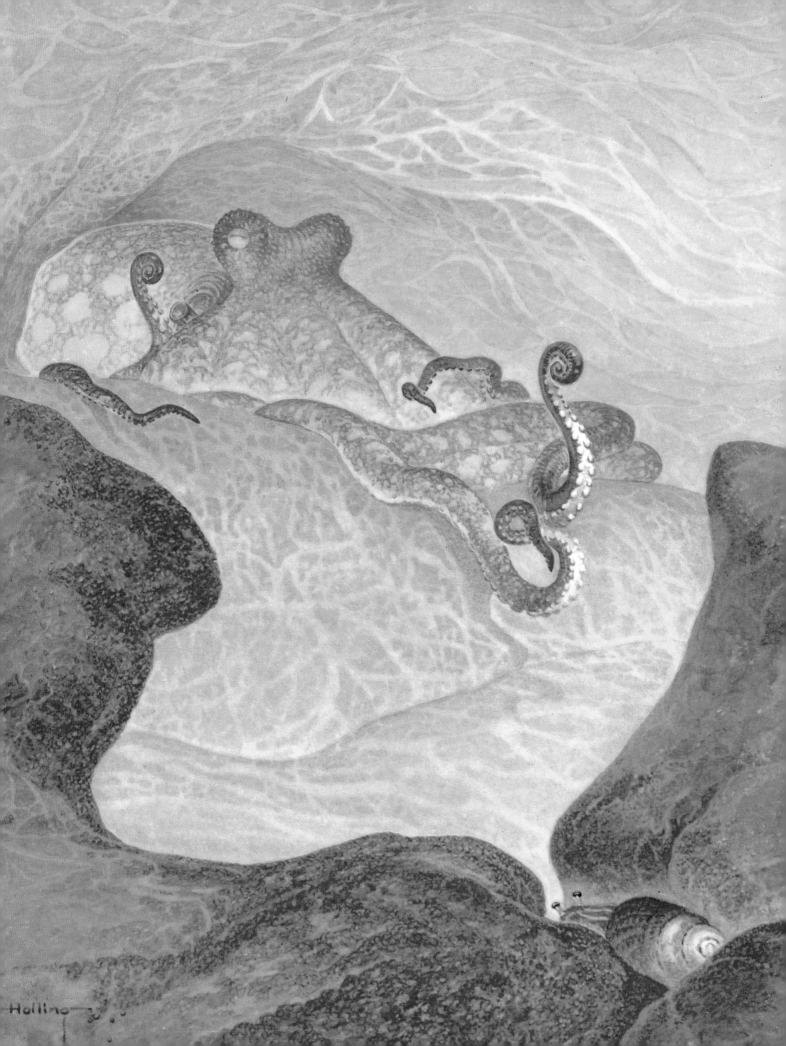

19. CAN THIS BE THE END OF PAGOO?

INSIDE his new shell, deep in his crack, down in the cave of Deep Hole, Pagoo was motionless. Both eye-stalks pointed toward the pale Octopus. This eight-armed Mollusk, this soft cousin of Mussels, Clams, and Oysters may not have seen Pagoo.

Of course she *could* have seen Pagoo. Now that her day's sleep had ended, she opened her soft, wrinkled eyelids. Her eyes were almost like human eyes, and her sight was keen, and hidden between those huge eyes lay a remarkable brain. Perhaps she had spied Pagoo from the first—had calmly watched him backing into the crack. *Perhaps* her Mollusk brain was planning tricks to play on this Crustacean.

With night, a weird cold light flooded Deep Hole. It was a night when sea fire danced on the surface and foaming waves flashed white lightning into the depths. Tiny luminous creatures swirled like fireflies, collected, crowded, and coated the rocks with silver. Their sparks showered down on the shell heap by the cave, and currents fanned the shells into glowing coals. The glow spread into the cave until the Octopus herself shone like a pale paper lantern. Pagoo watched her tentacles shimmering like ribbons.

Shuffling her tentacles, the Octopus slowly turned toward Pagoo. Small spurts of mud leaped from the floor as her body lifted and drifted toward his hiding place. She had pumped a few bursts of water through her funnel, the short pipe at her side. She could walk when she wished, or be jet-propelled—with speed.

Frightened Pagoo trembled. Her eyes! One of them surely spied him in his shell. Yet she wasn't attacking the little Hermit—she turned toward the cave door. Thin body-flaps hung down between tentacles in frilly folds. She shuffled outside like a little old lady, hunched in a floppy wrapper tied with too many cords. She did not even glance at Pagoo. He sagged, as though heaving a great sigh of relief.

"Don't relax!" hissed Old Instinct, and so Pagoo went rigid again. "Don t relax for a second. You *would* come here, and now you're trapped. One minute you're frightened to death—the next you think maybe you're not scared of this humble-looking lady. *Lady?* She's a WITCH! You watch out for her!"

This Witch of Deep Hole had a magic wand—at least it seemed to do magic things. She unrolled a tentacle and stretched it toward a rock two feet away. The rock gleamed with tiny bright lights, and its center held a cluster of stars. When the star cluster moved, Pagoo knew what it was—a Snail in its shell, busily grazing.

The Witch lifted and pointed her wand at the Snail. Goggle-eyed, Pagoo leaned forward until Old Instinct growled, "Get back inside!"

The tentacle was smooth as garden hose on top, but its under side was lumpy with "suckers." These suction cups looked like a double row of small white doughnuts. Now the tip of the Witch's wand plucked the shell from the rock. The Snail slammed its operculum door, but that would not help this doomed animal. It already was riding a conveyor-belt down the under side of the tentacle. One sucker stretched up like a rubbery tube-foot, took the shell from the curled tip, and waved it over to the next sucker in line. Like an old-fashioned bucket brigade, the suction cups stretched and passed the shell farther along in a steady, rippling movement. As the wand's tip explored for another morsel, Pagoo in his crack could look upward and see what became of the Snail.

While Pagoo stared, the Witch tilted backward a bit. Her tentacles spread from her body like the spokes of a wheel. The wheel's center hole was the mouth, which hid the only hard parts of an Octopus, its horny jaws. Upper and lower, they were the size and shape of a parrot's beak, but as yet, Pagoo had not seen those jaws.

The conveyor-belt brought the Snail near the Octopus' mouth. While a few suction cups clutched the shell, one or two others neatly sucked out the Snail. Then for an instant Pagoo saw the flash of the black, hooked beak. It killed the Snail. It tore the Snail apart, and the pieces vanished into the mouth. Meanwhile, using a tentacle as a broom, the Witch swept the empty shell outside to her trash heap. This lady was fussy about keeping her cave clean. She dumped out her victims' hard, bony remains.

Calmly the Witch stretched her wand toward another Snail. Pagoo simply could not stay here! Gingerly he put his feet down. He slid from the crack, tiptoed outside—and ran. He galloped and slid across the mud, he reached the steep rock leading up from Deep Hole, he climbed among little lights—and then looked down.

There she was below, looking up at him with those awful eyes. She had caught the second Snail while she watched Pagoo escaping. Perhaps it was all part of her fun to let him run and reach the rock before following in one jet-swift movement. A tentacle shot upward. Its tip lassoed Pagoo's shell—with Pagoo inside.

Still clutching Pagoo, the Witch let her lasso rest a moment. After all, this fat little Hermit Crab would have to wait his turn. She would hold him while she ran that last Snail through the finishing process. So far this evening, hunting had been good.

With that tentacle wrapped around his doorway Pagoo could not drop out and escape even if he had had the courage. From somewhere far inside, he heard a whisper.

"This looks like the ending, son. Sure does. In and out of a Sculpin was one thing—you stayed in one piece. But this Witch's beak sort of mangles things. I'm sad. Sad that Old Instinct won't advise your children, your children's children, while new ages roll and surge over new tide pools. I tried to pass along lessons learned by your ancestors. They learned them the hard way, son—and it wasn't too easy to send their lessons on to you. You wouldn't always listen; you thought you knew it all. And now the chain will be broken, and—well—goodbye. . . ."

8 2

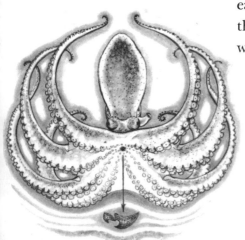

AN OCTOPUS HAS A
BEAK LIKE A PARROT'S

SHE LET HIM REACH THE ROCK BEFORE FOLLOWING.

ENDLESS RHYTHM OF AN OLD, OLD SEA

PAGOO did not travel on the underslung conveyor-belt. This time the Witch of Deep Hole crooked her arm and pointed his shell toward her mouth like a spoonful of dessert—*he* was the dessert!

Then something streaked through the water. Sharp jaws clipped the tentacle as if cutting a length of hose. The tentacle thrashed in the mud all by itself, as though it were a separate animal. The tip gripping Pagoo's shell opened out, the shell dropped, and Pagoo again could see. He saw the Moray Eel who had cut the tentacle making another swift charge. But where was the Octopus? She had jet-propelled herself to the cave like a flying missile. The Moray overtook her, and then. . . .

Pagoo was puzzled, because a great black cloud came boiling out of the cave. The Witch had emptied her ink sack. She had squirted ink for a "smoke screen," her last resort in time of trouble, and the Witch was in trouble! At the cave door a second tentacle writhed like a snake. So the Moray had found and clipped her again!

But no more. The Eel knew where the cave opened, he had seen her shoot into it, yet he blundered past as though he knew nothing at all. The ink not only clouded his eyesight, it seemed to spoil his sense of smell as well. He dashed about, lashing himself in aimless circles, mouth open. By chance his jaws slashed into the tentacle still flopping near the cave. This was his favorite food. He tore at it.

The Moray would not catch the Octopus again. Far back in her cave, in a narrow crack, she wriggled and squeezed and pressed her boneless body. Here she could hide until stumps of her two lost tentacles healed and grew out again, for that is the way of Witches and magic wands. At least, that is the way with Octopuses and tentacles.

Pagoo was free. He scuttled to the cliff and clambered up the sheer face of it without stopping. He made Mussel Ridge and Snail Cousins' Rock, dropped off a ledge and into an old Anemone, crawled out, and found his Grotto of Eating Trees.

Pagoo remained hidden and strangely quiet for a whole half-hour. Once again he had escaped the jaws of death, but he soon forgot about all that—it did not mean much. After all, death hangs around every corner of all tide-pool towns, its jaws are forever open.

"So you're still kicking!" grunted Old Instinct. "It's only luck—you did not escape by yourself. You learned nothing new, unless 'tis a fear of Octopuses. But shucks, that was learned by your great-grandfathers millions of generations back, and passed on to me, for you. Not my fault you muffed it. Well, we'll put down 'PAGOO'S ESCAPE FROM WITCH—NOTHING MUCH LEARNED.' But say—while you're in this grotto, notice the new shells rolled in by that storm—"

When morning washed over the rocks in sparkling foam, and fresh food from the deep was delivered to every door, Pagoo in a bright new shell went walking in Tide-pool Town. He broke through golden chains in the sea, let down by the sun, and he somehow seemed to be laughing at all chains. He ducked in time to let Big Head go banging along the ceiling, and thought nothing of it. He fought a most delightful scrap with a pair of bruisers, licked them both, and stopped to chop meat for the little fish around the corner. The Landlady edged her Traveling Towers up to the feed, and he let everyone dine free. Her look said, "My, what a smooth young chap! Now I wonder who . . . ." But Pagoo sat in his new shell, bowing, and cleaning his feelers.

"Maybe," said Old Instinct, "maybe, Pagoo, you'll grow all the way up, and have children, and—duck, son! Here's Big Head again."

Old Instinct was right. Pagoo did grow up, and he did have children. Though he never quite knew how, he heard an ancient call, *"Now is the time for new life to begin! Find yourself a mate!"*

Find a mate? He'd much rather sleep. . . . But then he saw HER.

There was little enough to see—merely the dainty tips of her feelers waving from a shell—but to Pagoo they were the loveliest feelers in all Tide-pool Town! He raced to her house and peered inside.

8 5

Away back in her pearly chamber her eyes glowed softly. Pagoo hammered her shell and seemed to yelp, "Come out here! Come *OUT!*"

She would not budge. A crowd of the biggest boys rushed Pagoo. Each felt that this young lady Hermit had waved at *him,* and produced fists to prove it. Pagoo licked them all, but they kept coming back. At last Pagoo hooked a thumb in his lady love's shell and dragged it beside him. The crowd stole her away, he yanked her back. . . .

Pagoo held to her house the longest. For three days and nights they became acquainted, gently patting each other. When one morning she molted and kicked her old crust out of the door, Pagoo brushed against her new skin, near the region of her heart.

He had left her with countless Seeds-of-Life, seeds too small for even a Hermit to see. They clung to the outside of her body, while within her lay hundreds of tiny eggs. Every egg held its own kind of built-in seed. Now each egg-seed *must* be found by one of Pagoo's seeds. On meeting, the two seeds would start building a new life in that egg—a little Pagurus would begin to grow.

"I'll watch over your mate," Old Instinct was saying. "She'll lay her eggs, and hang their clusters along her body. She'll rock gently inside her shell, swishing bubbly sea water around to clean and air those eggs. Oh, she'll make a wise mother, never fear. After many days, her children—and yours—will hatch out, and then . . . ."

IF HER SHELL HAD BEEN MADE OF GLASS,
SHE COULD HAVE BEEN SEEN CAREFULLY TENDING
HER SHINY CLUSTERS OF PURPLE EGGS

DAY BY DAY THE EGGS DEVELOPED.
IN EACH, A PAIR OF EYES APPEARED —
THEN A TINY HEART BEGAN TO BEAT.

AT LAST, FROM THIS BUNCH OF DOT-SIZED BALLOONS,
A NEW BABY PAGURUS WAS READY TO
H A T C H.

A glossy Pagoo, from an egg small as a pencil dot, drifted on the ocean. He heard the silent voice of Old Pal saying, "You're *hungry!*" And sure enough, he was. Once more a new Pagurus, Pagoo, for short, had found his place in the endless rocking rhythms of the sea.